Valerie Mendes was born in Buckinghamshire just after the Second World War began. She arrived too late to put a stop to it.

Educated at North London Collegiate School (which she loved) and the University of Reading (which she loathed) she was first published in her school magazine when she was six years old. It was a defining moment in her life.

During her many years in publishing, Valerie acquired a variety of nicknames. At Oxford University Press she was The Ogre Queen because she had inherited a list of Oxford Graded Readers. In one smaller and rather disorganised publisher she became known as Genghis Khan. While running Wordwise, her home-based freelance enterprise for eight years, everybody called her Eagle Eye.

In her private family life, Valerie is Mum to Sir Sam Mendes CBE and Granny Val to her beloved grand children.

Valerie is still a meticulous Editor, but now only has time for her own work. She has just completed *Finding My Voice: A Memoir* which is also published under her new imprint, VMBooks.

For further details, please see **www.valeriemendes.com**

Also by Valerie Mendes

For Paul Downes and Darren Millward
with gratitude and love

Victor hesitated at the door of the conservatory. 'Oh, and Beatrice ...'

She turned to look at him, 'Yes, dear?'

His eyes were very dark. 'Better luck next time?'

The flush of humiliation rose to her cheeks.

'Yes, Victor, of course ... Better luck next time.'

Beatrice

Beatrice Davenport looked at her reflection in the dressing-table mirror, her heart thundering with dread. She'd got used to being beautiful and now saw only her face and clothes as if they belonged to someone else.

She thought, I really don't know if I have the courage to go through with all this. It's finally Saturday the 7th of May 1910. I've been planning this morning for weeks, but now it's here I feel as frightened and desperate as a child who has lost her mother.

Her maid, Lisa, brushed Beatrice's long, dark-gold hair with practised strokes, electricity crackling beneath her fingers. The hair was piled, pinned, smoothed and fussed over, the curls at the neck immaculate. Beatrice, a perfectionist, checked her profile and found nothing out of place.

Slipping off her dressing gown, she stepped into a long petticoat, a swirling skirt, a tight-fitting jacket with pearl buttons. Pale grey and lilac, the outfit shimmered in the light, complimenting her flawless complexion and extraordinary violet eyes.

On went the hat, wide-brimmed, confident, made in the same colours, and crowned with a purple ostrich feather.

'You look particularly well this morning, ma'am.' Lisa stood back to admire her handiwork. 'Them colours suit you down to the ground ... Will you be needing anything else before you go?'

'No, thank you, Lisa.' Beatrice brushed away the specks of dust dancing on her shoulder. 'I'll be lunching in town.' She pulled on her cream leather gloves. 'Then I'll call in to see Miss Brightman to discuss some new designs. I'll be home for tea.'

'Yes, ma'am. Thank you, ma'am. It looks to be a lovely spring morning out there.'

How can it possibly be a lovely morning, Beatrice thought, when I so heartily want it to be over? During it I might – or might not – finally learn the truth about my condition. Except I don't want to hear it. I'd like to run away to a sandy beach and fling myself into the sea. Just imagine those waves. Their cool salty arms would close over me, no questions asked, their soothing voices singing in my head.

Yet look how carefully she'd planned every minute of this morning. The moment her husband, Victor, had said he'd be in Paris all weekend at a banker's conference, she'd seized the opportunity to arrange a special private consultation with the brilliant Dr Theodore Hertzler. On a Saturday morning when he'd have no other clients, no prying eyes or malicious gossips in his waiting room.

In St John's Wood, at the top of Clifton Hill, Beatrice hailed a hansom cab, drawn by a single horse.

'Harley Street, please, driver.' Her voice shook with anxiety.

The fragile sunshine made her blink. She slammed the cab door and sat against the stiff leather seat, drawing deep breaths. The smell of horse dung filled her head. It reminded her of their house, Chandos Manor, in Charlbury, a village in Oxfordshire – and Victor's beloved horses. How he adored the creatures! The hours he spent talking to them, riding his chosen gelding down through their gardens and out into the glorious expanse of surrounding countryside under an Oxfordshire sky…

The cab swayed and rumbled, jarring her spine. She raised her arms to steady her feathered hat and shut her eyes. She could still change her mind. Get out at Harley Street, but instead of going to the consulting rooms, she'd walk to Oxford Street, have a coffee at Debenham and Freebody. Then go to Liberty's to buy a roll of exotic silk or chiffon. Take it back to Hampstead to her beloved Laura, get out her sketch-pad and start drawing. Dr Hertzler would understand. She'd explain she'd changed her mind. Keep up the pretence there was nothing wrong.

Except she'd done exactly that for three years. Now really was the right time to face the truth. Courage, girl, courage. Theo might tell her she must simply be patient. Conceiving a child was miraculous, not something she could assume would happen overnight. She was only twenty-eight. Three years of trying for a baby was a drop in the ocean. Women often had to try for much longer. Unless they were Queen Victoria who had nine babies one after another and probably forgot their names.

It was the terrible *not knowing*. That feeling of failure clouding every thought and haunting every nightmare. She counted the days to her next period and then prayed it wouldn't happen … When it did, the worst part was having to tell Victor. Watch the disappointment kill his smile. Listen while he said, as he always did, *'Never you mind, my dear. Better luck next time.'*

Beatrice opened her eyes. The cab swung through the dusty streets. She glimpsed the trees in Regent's Park, the

3

startling green of their fresh spring leaves, the ravishing hands of pink and white blossom opening their fingers to the sky. How lucky they were. Their renewal so effortlessly guaranteed.

No, there was no getting away from it, not now she'd come this far. She *must* see Theo. Everyone said he was the best. Wonderful with women's troubles. Originally trained in New York, with masses of experience. A real gentleman.

And best of all, she knew him. He was one of their good neighbours in Charlbury, a great friend, often at their Chandos Manor table on a Saturday night. Out riding with Victor early on Sunday mornings, or fishing with him all day long in the River Evenlode. Which made it so much easier to talk to him.

Anything she told him would be treated in the strictest confidence. She'd never heard him so much as whisper about any of his other patients. And the *stories* he must have heard ... She could well imagine. The miscarriages, the venereal diseases, the back-street abortions. Thank God she wasn't complaining of any of those ... Be thankful for small mercies.

She forced herself into chintzy cheerfulness. Chin up, shoulders back. Lift your lips in a smile. Theo might become an earthbound angel and give her good news.

The cab lurched into Harley Street. She gathered up her long skirt, clambered out, and gave the driver his fare, her legs trembling. A smartly-dressed nurse pushing a large perambulator marched past. Beatrice peered quickly underneath the hood to glimpse the baby's face. She saw a softly rounded cheek, flushed with sleep; damp curls of copper-coloured hair. She caught the delicate scent of milk and talcum powder. Biting her lip until it bled, she watched as pram and nurse swung round a corner and disappeared.

If only the child belonged to her. *If only* ... Right, she'd do it. Now, this very minute. Summon up the courage, let the truth be told.

She climbed the steps of the consulting rooms and hung on to the bell.

Alexander

D r Alexander Hertzler heartily wished he were not clean-shaven. He could have used an enormous prickly puff of a moustache, a mighty waterfall of a beard to protect him from the cold. The bitter wind, laden with snow, drifted its way into his very bones, as if his fur-lined jacket, his cashmere scarf, the hood with ear-muffs and the leather gloves hung off his body in rags. Within minutes of climbing out of New York's subway, snow layered his thick black eyelashes and froze across his cheeks.

A silent white world and pitch-dark sky throbbed back at him.

He heard a growl. No, not a hungry dog. Only his empty stomach, grumbling.

He bent his head against the wind and stuffed gloved hands into his pockets, fighting exhaustion. He'd worked at St Luke's Hospital on 113th Street for seven days and nights, snatching a few hours' sleep in his Spartan living quarters only when his knees buckled and his eyelids drooped with weariness. The heavy rain last week had turned to hail and, in the afternoon, relentlessly heavy snow. Two of the hospital's ten house physicians had fallen sick. Covering for them, as well as doing his own job, had kept him permanently at his post. He'd coped with streams of emergencies as the victims of road accidents, shocked and bleeding, were wheeled in with broken bones and cracked skulls.

But today was Thanksgiving: Thursday, 24th November 1910. Nothing would stop him floundering home tonight for his special celebration supper: roast goose with stuffing, rich gravy and roast potatoes, followed by succulent plum pudding … His mouth watered.

In Greenwich Village, he turned the corner to his brownstone house, a gift from his in-laws on his marriage. His beautiful wife, Lillian, would be waiting for him, her eyes bright with welcome. Sylvia, their two-year-old daughter, would be tucked up in bed, fast asleep. He'd tiptoe into her room. It would be too late for lullabies, so he'd kiss the rounded warmth of her cheek, eat a glorious supper, drink a glass of wine – and revel in his own soft bed in Lillian's arms.

How he longed for them.

He reached his house, shoved impatiently at the metal gate. A heavy drift of snow lay against it. He frowned, pushing with all his strength, then raising his head. The steps to the front door looked like an unbroken white hill, as if nobody had climbed it for days. He started to brush away the snow, climbing each step, trying not to slip, slide and fall. If he broke any bones now, he'd be worse than useless. Damn the snow. It had brought down the telephone lines seven days ago. But he was sure Lillian had coped. She was so competent and organised. She could manage anything.

At the top of the steps, his jacket sopping wet, his knees frozen, he clumped the snow from his trousers, pulled off his gloves and fumbled stiff fingers for his key. The front door groaned beneath his touch.

He kicked it shut.

The hall sat in darkness. Silent shadows flickered in the living room.

He called, 'Hi, honey, I'm home! God, it's hell on earth out there! Come and give your frozen husband a kiss.'

No reply. He switched on a lamp and checked his watch. Five minutes past ten: later than he thought. Lillian must be asleep, worn out with waiting. He'd have to grovel apologies.

He unzipped his boots, walked down the hall to the kitchen and flung the door open. A stale smell wafted towards him. He switched on the light. Piles of dirty dishes littered the sink. Greasy pots sprawled on the draining board. The stone-cold oven's door gaped black and empty.

Thanksgiving supper?

This wasn't like his immaculate Lillian. Before they married in 1907, she'd been a Henry Street Settlement nurse on New York's Lower East Side, where five hundred thousand people were packed into an area no larger than a mid-sized Kansas farm. A single city block might house three thousand residents. Lillian spent her days in the squalid tenements caring for the sick, often paying more than eight visits a day, scuttling up and down the stairs in her starched blue uniform, dodging the rats, crunching the cockroaches or, in the heat of summer, stepping across the baking rooftops as a welcome short cut.

'Our poverty-stricken tenement dwellers have every disease you can name,' she told him that first night they met, she in her turquoise-silk party frock, her dark hair coiled and shining. 'Pneumonia, dysentery, thrush, whooping cough, scarlet fever, tonsillitis, rheumatism, tuberculosis, eye diseases, ulcers, meningitis … I've looked after them for five years and I've never even caught a sore throat. I believe passionately in cleanliness. Wherever I go – if I can, if there's clean water – I wash my hands and every surface I touch.'

Lillian would never allow her own kitchen to get into this filthy mess. Their cleaner, Elsa, must have been trapped in her lodgings by the snow.

He managed to find a clean glass, filled it with water and gulped it down. At least the pipes weren't frozen … He'd love a stiff whisky. He'd wake Lillian, see if she wanted supper. They'd wash the dishes together before bed. He longed to sleep for a week, but he had to be back at St Luke's in the morning.

He padded silently upstairs. The bathroom door stood open. Another vile smell gusted out at him: old pea soup. The lavatory was full of dark green stools. He flushed the toilet, feeling nauseous.

What in goddam's name is wrong?

He passed Sylvia's door without looking in on her. In his bedroom the lamplight cast long shadows. The bed linen looked damp and rumpled. The heavy stink of sweat rolled towards him.

Lillian paced up and down the far side of the room, wringing her hands. Her hair tumbled down her back. Her flimsy nightgown clung to her limbs.

'Lillian? My darling girl!' Alex leaped across the room and took her in his arms.

Her skin felt burning hot. 'What in God's name has happened?'

'It's the mountain.' Her breath beat against his face. 'I have to climb the mountain to reach the light, but every time I try, the vicious wind blows like a giant bear, huffing and puffing, pushing me off.'

'What *are* you on about?' God Almighty, Lillian was delirious. He held her at arms' length. 'You have a fever. You should be in bed.'

'Ah, yes, Alex.' Lillian's eyes focused. 'You're back at last! The snow … White, freezing, ghastly … On and on it came. We've had no telephone for days. The lines are cut to shreds … I must tell you … So important … Something you need to know.'

He encouraged her towards the bed. 'Just you rest now, darling girl. Here, lie down … I'll fetch you something to drink –'

'No, I need to tell you quickly, before I get worse.'

Lillian slumped on to the pillows. Her gown gaped open. Her breasts and abdomen were covered in rose-coloured spots.

Alex's heart throbbed with a terrible recognition. 'What is it? Tell me.'

'Sylvia's dead. Our baby. Our darling little girl. She died last night. Or the night before. I can't remember. I've lost count.'

'*What?*'

'I did my best, darling. I fought so hard. I tried everything. It wasn't my fault. She had typhoid fever. She gave it to me. Or I gave it to her. I don't know, it all happened so fast.' Lillian began to sob. 'She's in her room. I laid her to rest but she wants to see her very special dad to say goodbye.'

Alex hurtled from the room, his breath stabbing his ribs.

Sylvia lay in bed. He placed his hand against his daughter's cheek. Cold as ice. He felt for a pulse. None. With a thud, her arm flopped back on the sheet as he let it go.

Great God in heaven … Lullabies? … He'd never sing to her again.

A sound escaped him: a cry, a groan, a sob, a shout of

denial, as if it gushed from somebody else's throat. The walls seemed to close around him as he slumped to the floor, retching lumps of sick from an empty stomach.

He regained consciousness, feeling faint. He hauled himself to his feet and staggered back to his bedroom. Up and down, up and down, Lillian paced like a demented ghost.

Once again, he caught her in his arms. 'I can't *believe* – ' He couldn't say the words. 'How did you *get* into such a state? How can I help? What can I *do*?'

'Nothing.' Lillian slumped against him. 'Too late. Nothing.'

'Nonsense.' He picked her up and carried her to bed. 'There must be *some*thing you can take. Lie there, now … I'll find it.'

He tore into the bathroom, opened the cabinet above the sink. It was stuffed with packets and bottles. He lifted them out, hurling them into the bowl. Castor oil, listerine, flaxseed meal, arnica, mustard leaves, tablets of quinine, essence of peppermint, lavender salts, iodine, laudanum, oil of clove, calomel.

All utterly useless.

He crashed back to the bedroom. Lillian lay so still beneath the quilt his heart rose to his throat. 'I can't find anything.' He perched beside her. 'How did it happen? When did it begin?'

Lillian licked her lips and tried to swallow. She held out a hand. 'Your birthday party.'

'But that was three weeks ago.' His mind spun with disbelief. 'What's that got to do with anything?'

'I hired a cook – '

'That pretty Irish lass. Salads, pies, cold meats. Delicious – '

'She was a good cook, Alex … And also a carrier.'

'Of typhoid?' His body stiffened with fury. 'Are you *sure*?'

'Positive. Some of our friends have the same symptoms. Two of them rang before the lines went down. Lulu and Mike … Angelica and – '

'Lillian! My God, darling! What have we done?'

'It's not our fault. It's not anyone's fault – '

'But the girl … She must be traced.'

'No, Alex, *no*.' Her hand gripped like a vice. 'She'll have heard the rumours and vanished. It's much too late for Sylvia. And now it's too late for me.'

'Don't talk nonsense. Of course it isn't.'

His exhaustion and hunger had vanished. He was a doctor. He'd take over and put everything right. 'We'll get you to St Luke's. I'll ring for an ambulance.'

'You can't. The lines are down.' Her hand slithered from his. 'I don't want to go anywhere. Just stay with me.' She looked away. 'The light behind the mountain comes closer every minute. It's pale blue, and wonderfully bright. Stay with me, please, until I pass away.'

'For God's *sake*, Lillian. Don't talk so. I'll not give up on you, not in a thousand years.'

He leaped to his feet. In a trice he was out of the room, down the stairs, through the hall. He wrenched at the front door. A wave of icy air burst on to his face. He stood on the steps, his legs shaking with panic.

He shrieked to the dark street and the silent drifts of snow. *'Help! Help me! My wife, she's very ill. So ill, she might die.'* The silence intensified, beating on his ears.

'In the name of God, will somebody please help!'

Beatrice

'As far as I can tell, Beatrice,' Dr Theo Hertzler smiled, his tanned skin creasing seductively around his dark brown eyes, 'there's nothing wrong with you.' His rich American drawl seemed out of place in the ferocious neatness of his consulting room: too warm and reassuring, its tone too full of honey for the confines of its walls. 'For a twenty-eight-year-old woman you're in peak physical condition.'

She flushed with surprise. 'God, that's music to my ears.'

She'd dressed as fast as she could. Now her hat and gloves lay on her knees, her hair tumbled to her shoulders. She still felt Theo's cool fingers on her body. 'I've been imagining a hundred terrible things.'

'I'm sure you have. People do. They worry themselves into the ground and then wonder why they don't enjoy making love any longer!' Theo glanced down at his notes. 'May I ask you a few questions?'

'Of course.' She slid her hands beneath her hat and clenched her fists, desperately hoping he wouldn't ask about her past.

'Have you ever taken drugs of any kind for your infertility?'

'No. Nothing. Not a single pill.' At least *that* was the truth.

'I'm delighted to hear it. Secret diseases breed horrible secret remedies. There are hundreds of quacks in this country of yours who'll sell you everything from mercury, ointments, injections and pills to poultices and emetics. Who recommend courses of bleeding and dangerous surgery. None of which make *my* job any easier.'

'The only remedy I've ever swallowed was a so-called tonic made by a Lydia Pinkham. I spotted her advertisement in a magazine. She described the mixture as an elixir with "a baby in every bottle". I ordered three bottles and drank every drop. It tasted disgusting, of roots and mildew. And of course it was worse than useless.'

'I could have told you that before you drank it!'

The warmth and laughter in Theo's voice made her smile back.

'Have you and Victor ever practised birth control?'

'No. Victor and I always wanted to have children. He bought Chandos Manor before we met and spent a lot of money renovating it. Now it's an ideal family home, as you know, with rooms that should be nurseries, play rooms, school rooms. Except they stand empty.'

'Could your sterility be Victor's fault? Ideally, in cases such as yours, I'd prefer to see you both.'

'He'd never agree to it, Theo. He has no idea I'm seeing you and I have no intention of telling him. Anyway, Victor's one of the healthiest men I've ever met. He's forty but he looks younger. He has boundless energy. He does the work of three directors at his bank, and he's never ill.'

'Hmm.' Theo's eyes clouded over. 'Testing sperm is a relatively simple procedure.'

'But I'm sure it's my fault!'

'You might have a slight inflammation of the pelvic

region. Or you could have blocked Fallopian tubes. I can't tell for certain until I perform surgery – '

'No!' She bit her lip. 'I'm not going under the knife. I'd never manage to keep *that* a secret.'

Theo put down his pen. 'Then we'll have to find another way.'

Her heart thudded. 'You mean there *might* be a solution?'

'I can't give you any guarantees, Beatrice, but we could start with your lifestyle … Take me through what you do in an average week.'

'Well, I work at my dressmaking business full-time five days a week from my house in Hampstead. Laura Brightman has been my partner since we both left The Slade. We set up *A Passion for Fashion* together and now employ four girls. I do the designing, Laura makes the first of the dresses and if it's a success the girls take over. I absolutely love it. Apart from the thrill of seeing my designs in action on other women, the Hampstead house is my real home. It's where I was born. Laura bought the house next door and we've linked the houses together. When Victor asked me to marry him, I agreed on condition that I could keep the business running.'

'But you also organise his house in St John's Wood – and Chandos Manor.'

'He has servants, Theo. Victor makes sure I'm well looked after. We may entertain every week but I don't cook for his dinner parties. I'm just there as a guest.'

'Hardly, Beatrice. You're an elegant and accomplished hostess. You're running the show. Organising the staff, planning the menus, making sure your guests are happy … Making sure Victor is happy.' Theo looked her squarely in the eyes. 'You're on call the whole time, aren't you? You're never off the hook.'

She crossed her legs. 'Well, if you put it like that, I suppose I am. But I enjoy being busy. I love the pulse of London life. I like its demands.'

'You may like it, but maybe your body's telling you to slow down.'

'You mean, do less of everything?'

'I'm suggesting you spend more time in the country and less at work. Make Mondays and Tuesdays your Charlbury days on your own. Then join Victor and Laura in London for the rest of the week and travel to Charlbury with your husband on Friday evenings. Take regular gentle country exercise. Give up tea, coffee and alcohol. Have a siesta in the afternoon. Spend more time with Victor without any dinner party guests. And when you *are* in bed with him, stop worrying and enjoy it. Above all, be patient.'

'The trouble is, Theo, I'm not a country woman. I don't ride – I find side-saddle uncomfortable – I don't fish, I'm not a gardener. I don't shoot grouse or hunt foxes. I hardly know anyone in Charlbury – and I'm not at all sure that Laura would agree to run our business with so much of it on her shoulders.'

Theo pushed at his chair and stood at the window. 'But you came here to consult me.' He looked back at her. 'Imagine how wonderful it would be if you took my advice, and conceived a child.'

She stood on the steps of Harley Street, taking gulps of air, dizzy with relief and hope. She'd thanked Theo, pinned up her hair and secured her hat. He refused her offered fee. She promised him unlimited Charlbury suppers, wanting to hug him for being so courteous and encouraging.

The bright morning sunshine had vanished into a faint refreshing rain that dampened the pavements and settled the dust. Her mind whirled with Theo's suggestions. She'd think them over, discuss them with Laura, and eventually tell Victor she had new plans.

But a few minutes later, she realised any immediate decision would have to wait. The newspaper vendor at the end of the street was yelling his lungs out.

'Read all about it! The King is dead! Edward the Seventh died last night. His majesty is dead. Long live George the Fifth! Long live the King!'

She bought a damp newspaper, its headlines dancing before her eyes. So … Everyone would go into mourning for the monarch they called Edward the Caresser. With his voracious appetite for vast meals, voluptuous women and fat cigars, he'd brought a louche vitality to court life, unthinkable in his mother's reign. When Queen Victoria died in January 1901, the entire nation looked like a flock of despondent crows. Now, every fashionable woman in London would clamour for a new black suit and evening wear to match.

A Passion for Fashion would be in overdrive.

She flung out an arm to hail another cab.

'Could you take me to the centre of Hampstead, please? As quickly as you can.'

Alexander

Nobody heard him shrieking into the drifts of falling snow – and nobody came to his door.

He sat with Lillian all night, struggling to get her temperature down, encouraging her to drink boiled water with slices of lemon. Telling her how much he loved her, she must stay alive for him, they were going to be all right, they would have another daughter, more children.

By dawn, although still weak as a kitten, Lillian's forehead felt cooler to his touch and she'd stopped jabbering about the mountain.

For a few hours, utterly exhausted, he slept with his arms around her. At midday he gave her a bath, made her drink a bowl of nourishing soup. He changed the sweat-drenched bed-linen, dusted and tidied the room. By early evening, he knew she had survived the worst.

Thank God. His one and only Lillian would live.

'In the deepest grief there is no weeping.'

He remembered those words many times during the weeks that followed when, longing to cry for his dead Sylvia, his eyes remained dry as dust. The words were what his father used to say, and he sure knew. He was the best country doctor Alex ever saw, he reckoned that Kansas had ever seen. He'd died five years ago, and Alex never missed him so much as he did at his little daughter's funeral.

The snowy remnants of that fatal blizzard still lay everywhere, hard and slippery, glittering in the grey air, bitter reminders.

When the funeral was over, he and Lillian returned to the silence of their empty house, the sound of sobbing heavy in their ears. They had nothing to say to each other but meaningless platitudes. Lillian's parents could hardly bear to look at him.

'When you married my daughter,' her father told him through clenched teeth, his eyes red, his face gaunt with weeping, 'my only child, my most precious darling girl, we *assumed* you'd be a safe pair of hands. Young doctor, good at caring for people, always knew the right thing to do. We hoped you'd look after our Lillian. *Now* look what you've done. Neglected her and allowed our only grandchild to pass away … We'll never forgive you.'

He tried to tell the bitter old man he was desperately sorry. Sylvia's death had pretty much sapped the will to live out of him too. He'd battled for Lillian's life that snowbound night, tooth and claw. Nobody could have fought harder. If it hadn't been for his own immaculate care, she'd also be dead.

But the old man turned away, his eyes full of loathing. He knew his father-in-law never wanted to see him again.

Lillian agreed he should go back to work. Everyone at St Luke's had heard their news. They were sympathetic, but too busy for more than a few comforting words. He took refuge in the hectic routine. For at least five minutes, it let him forget that tiny coffin.

With humiliating desperation, he tried to talk to Lillian. He invited her to dinner. She refused. She said it would be pointless, she had no appetite. Over Christmas, he offered to take her on holiday, wherever she chose, anywhere in the world. Lillian didn't want to leave New York. Every night, Alex asked her what *she'd* done during the day. Lillian shrugged. She couldn't remember. The house was spotless, airless and meaningless. Everything sat in its proper place, silent as the tomb.

He lacked the courage to walk into Sylvia's nursery. When he held Lillian in his arms in bed at night, longing for warmth and comfort, she froze and slid away. When he woke, the other side of their bed gaped empty as a toothless mouth. Lillian lay in the spare room, a bottle of sleeping pills beside her, the pillow still damp with tears.

One evening in the middle of January, he got home to find Lillian waiting for him in the hall, wearing her hat, coat and shiny shoes. Two new suitcases bulged on the floor beside her.

She said, 'I'm sorry, I can't stand the silence.' She stared fixedly ahead. 'I can't bear living each day without Sylvia. I've no one to care for. Father thinks I'm making myself ill. He's taking Mother and me to Europe. France, Italy, frankly anywhere that doesn't remind me of my darling little girl. Until the spring … I may be home then. Look after yourself, Alex. I do love you. I'm very sorry, but I … But I can't … Goodbye.'

And she was gone.

He stood there, staring at the door. Then he crumpled to

his knees. Strangled cries burst from his mouth like mice escaping a trap.

He couldn't bear to be alone in their brownstone house. Every nook and cranny seemed full of Sylvia's ghost. The kitchen rang with her laughter. He could see her eating in her high chair, waving her spoon, chocolate dessert smeared around her mouth. She'd taken her first steps in the living room, tottering towards him as he held out his arms, her eyes shining. He'd sung her to sleep in the nursery with her favourite lullabies. She'd bump down the stairs on her bottom, step by step, concentrating, solemn with purpose, gleeful with triumph. She'd splashed bubbles into his face in the bathroom, balanced her wooden boats, gurgling with watery happiness.

He gave Elsa, their cleaner, a stash of dollars and a glowing reference. He'd be living mostly at the hospital in future, working around the clock. There was little point in her caring for an empty house. She burst into tears, but Alex shut the front door before he changed his mind.

The only way he could cope with the pain was to work.

So there he was: always available at St Luke's, day and night, at everyone's beck and call. Never saying no to an out-patient, an emergency, an operation. Going home every ten days for one miserable night, to pay the bills, make sure the place hadn't burned to the ground.

Not that he'd have given a dime if it had.

One Saturday morning in early February 1911, he got a letter from his brother. He recognised the writing immediately. As a child, Theo, seven years his elder, clever, handsome and miraculously articulate, had been his absolute hero, the person he wanted to emulate, the boy and then the man he adored.

He took the letter into the kitchen and made a cup of strong, sweet coffee. He stared at the envelope, not wanting to reveal its message. He turned it over and tried to pretend he'd never received it.

But that didn't work. What if Theo were ill? Or married? What if …

His hands shook as he opened the envelope, his eyes blurred over the words. He was much more exhausted than he realised.

The Cottage, Church Street,   *28 January 2011*
Charlbury, Oxfordshire

My dearest Al,

I was devastated to hear your news. I hope you will forgive me for not leaping to your rescue and coming to see you and Lillian as soon as I could. Believe me, I had the best of intentions. I'd even booked my passage.

But the fates decided otherwise. I collapsed with a bad dose of influenza, which has been doing the seasonal rounds here. My London housekeeper insisted I stay in bed, and I couldn't throw off the infection. The minute I recovered, I had a host of delayed operations to cram into my hospital schedule, and a hundred ailing ladies needing me in Harley Street.

I only managed to get down to my blissful country retreat last night. It has snowed for a week and everything looks beautiful, so clean and fresh. It's such a relief to have a few quiet days to myself.

You know that alas! I've not yet met Lillian and never had the good fortune to see your little girl. I can only imagine your heartbreak. You're a fine, upstanding young man, and you don't deserve to be dealt such a cruel hand. I can only imagine what it must be like to lose someone so very dear and close.

But your life must go on. You and Lillian must have another beautiful daughter, a handsome son. I know you will continue your excellent work at St Luke's and that you will not let what has happened stand in the way of your career and ambitions.

And here's my suggestion. In the spring, you and Lillian must take a vacation. Give yourselves a real breather. Step on to an ocean liner and come to see your devoted brother in England. I'll be only too delighted to pay for the trip, and I'm sure St Luke's will give you compassionate time off.

While you are here, you and Lillian can explore London at your leisure. There's so much to see. I'll drive you both down to Charlbury. We can ride together over the green fields and beyond. Two good friends of mine, Beatrice and Victor Davenport, own Chandos Manor, the other side of the church yard here in Charlbury. They have excellent steeds you can borrow for as long as your hearts desire. I'm sure Lillian can ride – and if she can't, you must teach her. There's nothing quite like a gallop over Oxfordshire's fields with the wind in your hair and the clouds high in the sky to blow away the cobwebs in your mind.

Talk it over with Lillian, say yes and name the day! I'm so looking forward to meeting her and of course to seeing you again, my dearest brother.

Meanwhile, roll on the spring. You are often in my thoughts. I wish Pa were alive so you could share your sorrows with him.

I send you all my love. I'll write to you again as soon as I can.

Your ever loving brother
Theo

Alex read the letter twice, his hands shaking.

Fury surged through him like a river of fire. What in the *hell* did Theo know? They hadn't seen each other since Pa's funeral, five years ago. Patronising! Infuriating! Smug, self-

23

satisfied bastard! Lillian this, Lillian that. He knew *nothing*. Never even *met* her for Christ's sake. Never married. Never had kids. All leather gloves and Harley Street ladies in their lace bonnets with too much money to burn and nothing seriously wrong with them. Weekends in the boring English countryside sitting by the river with his posh English chums. Enough to make a hard-working fellow like himself puke into his boots.

But the inky words stabbed at him. As if his know-it-all brother had seared through his heart with his clever surgeon's knife and left it, split and bleeding on his kitchen table. How he'd managed to make everything a darn sight worse.

Tears burned his eyes. He crushed the pieces of paper into a damp ball, stumbled out of the kitchen, climbed the stairs to the attic. He lurched towards the window and flung it wide.

Bitter February air gusted into his face. Grit chewed at his eyeballs. He smoothed the ball into its semi-original state, ripped the letter deliberately and tidily into as many shreds as he could manage.

Then he threw them out.

The wind dipped and swelled.

It took the tiny pieces and they fluttered to the sky.

That afternoon he started to drink.

He was on his own. Nobody cared about him or what he did. Who could blame him? He used to have a life. Now he only had patients who sucked the energy out of him and hardly ever said a word of thanks.

Unusually, he'd taken the weekend off. The other doctors insisted. Indeed, they'd practically pushed him out the door.

Len Grant said, 'For God's sake, Al. Take a proper

breather. You're pretty much dead on your feet. You'll make one terrible mistake with that surgeon's knife if you don't go home *right this very minute*. I won't listen to any excuses. Get some shut eye, big time.'

He and Len were friends. Real pals, like the best of brothers. They'd known each other since medical school. For years, they'd shared an apartment given to Len by his wealthy father, who made sure the boys ate properly and had decent boots to wear. They knew each other inside out. He saw the rare but frosty warning light in Len's eyes and gave in.

Just for a few hours, then. See you Monday sharp.

He tried to make detailed plans, so every minute would be accounted for, leaving him no time to brood. He meant to walk in Central Park – something he, Lillian and Sylvia had done so many times together.

He wasn't a husband or a father now, just a solitary, haggard-looking singleton. He'd avoid looking at couples laughing into each other's eyes, pushing their buggies, holding their toddlers' hands, playing ball and bowling hoops. He'd shut his ears to the happiness in their voices.

After his walk, he'd have an evening meal. Order a luscious steak with fries, a chocolate ice-cream with fat buttery cookies. He'd go to a nickelodeon theatre whose ten-cent programme would include a slapstick comedy – he'd clean forgotten how to laugh. A Western with all those massive horses. And a travelogue – when had he last been anywhere?

They'd be something to talk about at St Luke's that had nothing to do with out-patients, infections, epidemics, gut rot and chickenpox. He'd gotten so out of touch with the world, he'd become dull as ditch water.

But when it came down to it, he did nothing.

He'd slammed the window shut and stomped downstairs, wiping his face on his sleeve. He gulped his cold coffee and opened a bottle of whisky. He'd have a thumbnail of liquor to perk himself up. He needed the energy to get as far as Central Park.

When he woke, he'd slumped on to the kitchen table, staring at a smeared glass and an empty bottle. It was Sunday midday. His head thundered like an angry storm, every bone in his body ached and his mouth tasted of pitch.

He staggered up to the bathroom where he was sick as a dog. He soaked in a hot tub, slept all afternoon, put on clean clothes and went back to St Luke's with nothing to talk about and everything to hide.

Thank you so much for your lovely letter, dearest Theo, how kind of you to write.

He'd packed a bag with fresh underwear, professionally laundered shirts, several pairs of socks – and an unopened bottle of liquor. He'd bought it in a job lot for that fatal birthday party. It wasn't whisky or wine or gin. Colourless and odourless, this alcohol left no tell-tale smell on the breath.

It was vodka.

He reasoned with himself as he left the house. He'd only take a small nip when he'd finished his shift. He didn't even enjoy the stuff. He'd never been a drinker. His Pa would explode with rage when he'd had to clean up the handiwork of some neighbouring doctor who'd been drunk as a coot while operating. He'd warned him so many times.

'*Lay off the liquor, son. It can put your work in jeopardy, wreck your marriage and destroy your liver. Who needs it? Keep it for a special treat, like on Thanksgiving.*'

Occasionally, he and Lillian had shared a bottle of wine

over supper. He loathed brandy and gin. Whisky was his tipple, but it might make his breath smell. So vodka it would be. Only now and then. When he felt especially tired. To help him forget Sylvia's death and Lillian's departure. To help him kill those memories in sleep.

He reached St Luke's and his living quarters. He slid the bottle into the back of his chest of drawers. Nobody would find it there. Anyway, he'd be so busy over the next ten days he'd probably forget about it.

But he didn't.

First he took a nip mid-afternoon, when his energies began to flag, to spur himself on. He drank half a tumbler before he went to sleep. He began to use it to help himself wake up, his head throbbing, his tongue rough as sandpaper.

When he finished the first bottle – and then the second – he could think of nothing but replacing them. He made an excuse to take a walk at lunchtime, dash into the nearest store, buy another bottle and smuggle it into St Luke's inside his coat. He felt guilty in a grubby kind of way – but not so strongly that it stopped him in his tracks.

It took something really serious for *that*.

It was nine in the morning.

He'd woken three hours before, remembering it was February 14th 1911: Valentine's Day. But he had nobody in his life waiting patiently at the window for his message of love, his bunch of roses. Hell, he didn't even know where in the world Lillian *was*. Paris or Rome or Madrid?

He was about to perform a tricky operation to remove a large ovarian cyst from an overweight forty-year-old woman. He'd drunk half a bottle of vodka the night before and almost finished the rest the moment he woke.

As he stood there staring at his knife, his legs began to shake. Then his whole body trembled, desperate to sink to the floor. His eyes blurred. All he could see was a grey mist and a swirl of dangerous shadows. He put down the knife before he blacked out.

They scraped him off the disinfected linoleum. He gained consciousness and shook his colleagues away – his assistant surgeon, the experienced anaesthetist, the anxious nurses. He told them he had influenza, but he couldn't get his tongue to work properly. He made slurring noises, coughed, laughed and pretended to sneeze. He noticed they shot worried glances at one another.

They packed him off immediately.

Len said, 'Go take a rest, Al … Get over that flu of yours. We don't want to catch it, nor do your patients!'

On his way to Greenwich Village, delivery boys dashing about with bouquets, chocolates and silly smiles on their chubby little faces, he bought six bottles of whisky.

They clanked together in their brown paper bag as he clumped up the steps of his house and slammed the door.

Beatrice

Beatrice reached her house in Hampstead's Elm Row, glad to be out of the dust and drizzle of central London.

She gazed lovingly up at it as she walked along the gravel path to the front door. It was and always would be her real home. She might live as Victor's wife in St John's Wood and Charlbury, but those addresses were his properties, not hers. Apart from her choice of Lisa as her personal maid in London – she insisted on managing without one in Charlbury – all the servants were Victor's appointments. Both houses had been furnished to his taste, and their domestic routines established, long before her arrival.

She often felt superfluous to requirements. Although they sometimes shared a bed, Victor had his own bedrooms in both houses. Breeding his children would have brought them so much closer. He was a man used to controlling every aspect of his life and those around him. Getting his own way in almost everything.

Except for this.

She had a thousand happy memories of her Elm Row front garden. The top windows at the back of the house looked over

Hampstead Heath, but there was no private garden behind it. Here, in the front, secluded by dense hedges within the narrow lane, when they were children, she'd played ball and bowled her hoop with her older sister, Miriam. She'd sat over Indian tea and Victoria sponge with her father after Miriam had married and left home: she with her sketch-pad on her knees, her father carefully thumbing one of his treasured first editions.

After she'd met Laura Brightman, a fellow student, at their art college, The Slade, she'd brought her back for supper and shown her the house. Then, weeks later, she'd met Laura's brother, the photographer Ralph Brightman, in the most extraordinary evening of her life. Later still, she'd proudly introduced him to her father, watched them talk and laugh together.

The two men in her life she'd loved the most.

Now, both of them were dead: Ralph in that tragic accident on a foggy winter's night, her father three months later. Only her beloved Laura remained: her best friend, closer than her own sister, a real companion. And now a sturdy, unflappable, enthusiastic business partner and an ally in matters large and small.

She remembered, on her wedding day, how Laura had stood beside her as her Matron of Honour, organising Miriam's ten-year-old twins as page boys and Miriam's thirteen-year-old daughter, Charlotte, as bridesmaid. Laura smoothed her ankle-length skirt and adjusted her veil. Beatrice had designed her own dress – high-necked and long-sleeved. Laura had made it out of cream satin with an overlay of delicate lace, embroidering it at the neck and wrist with exquisite clusters of pearls.

'You must be the most beautiful bride in the world.' Tears of love and admiration stood in Laura's eyes. 'I hope Victor realises he's a *very* lucky man.'

Laura was the only person she'd told about her consultation with Dr Theo Hertzler. She'd be longing to hear what had happened in Harley Street.

Laura looked across at her as she walked into the ground-floor room of the adjoining house. During the week, this was where their four girls sat at their Singer sewing machines, material whirring beneath their skilful fingers. Laura wore a neat cotton navy-blue dress, her sleek dark hair parted in the middle and coiled at the nape of her neck. She'd never known Laura to look anything but polished, elegant, stylish but understated.

A bale of black silk lay beside her on the long work table.

'Hello, darling.' Laura gestured towards the silk. 'Have you heard? We now have a new King, and go into mourning for at least six weeks. It's *such* a pity. We've produced some glorious summer dresses in every colour under the sun, but nobody will be allowed to wear them until 1911.'

'The Queen will probably wear black for an entire year!' She sank into the nearest chair. 'I've just read all about it in *The Times.*'

'We've had a dozen phone calls in the last hour and now we're fully booked all next week.' Laura grimaced. 'I know it's good for business so I suppose I shouldn't grumble. There'll be an enormous funeral with all the trimmings, and next year we'll have to make dozens of frocks for the Coronation. How the Royal family keep us dressmakers busy as bees! … Now, tell me. How did you get on with Theo?'

The telephone rang in her study. She stood up.

'I'll answer that. I'll make us something to eat and we can talk.'

They sat over bowls of celery soup, slices of fresh white bread and chunks of cheddar cheese.

'Theo was kind, considerate, encouraging and firm. He says there's nothing physically wrong with me, but he wants me to slow down. Do less work here with you, less entertaining with Victor's guests, generally less of everything that isn't going to help me conceive ... Obviously we'll all need to work flat out for the next few months, which will take us into early autumn.'

'And *then* what?'

'We'll both have to do a lot of thinking and planning.' Beatrice hesitated. 'The last thing I want is to sit around Chandos Manor twiddling my thumbs while Victor's on his own in London and you're coping valiantly without me. But maybe we could all manage perfectly well if I stayed in Charlbury on Mondays and Tuesdays. I could take the early train to London on Wednesday mornings and come straight here. And of course, I'd have lots of time to work on my designs in the conservatory at Chandos Manor. It's a gloriously quiet and inspiring place to think and draw.'

'And that would still leave you three days every week to see our clients. As long as it isn't any less, I think the new routine could succeed. We'll have to plan our diaries very carefully.'

'I'd telephone you every day from Chandos. If there's an emergency, I can reach you in a couple of hours. The proof of this particular pudding will be in its eating. We can experiment with the new schedule in the autumn and see whether it works ... in every possible way.'

She spent an hour after lunch working on designs for a smart day suit in black linen with a narrow skirt and long tight jacket. By three o'clock she'd had enough. She flung down her pencils and went to find Laura, who was putting the finishing touches to a glamorous evening dress for one of their most demanding clients.

'Can I tempt you to a walk on the Heath? I told Lisa I'd be back for tea, but I'd love to get some fresh air before I go back to stuffy old St John's Wood.'

'Good idea.' Laura put down her needle and thread. 'I can finish this tomorrow in a couple of hours. I could probably be accused of working too hard anyway. I need to take a leaf from your book!'

'It's a real problem, isn't it? Living and working in the same place, you never get away. At least I can escape to St John's Wood, even if there are times when I'd much rather be here with you.'

'But you do still love your husband.' Laura looked her in the eye. 'Straight answer, please. What are you telling me?'

She flushed. 'I like Victor very much. I respect him for his energy and vigour, for his confidence. He's kind and generous, he supports my working here, I'm proud to be at his side when we entertain his important banking friends.'

'Very good, my lord … Well defended. But …'

'There's a difference between loving someone as a friend and companion – and being madly in love. The difference becomes a gap that grows a fraction wider every day. I can only watch it grow in a helpless, hopeless way. Like there's a river running between us, forcing us to go our separate ways.'

'Did Theo ask you whether you loved your husband?'

'No, darling. And thank God he didn't. Theo has to assume the couples he sees want children because they enjoy being together. He's not a marriage counsellor.'

'And he didn't ask you whether you'd ever been in love with anybody else?'

'No, and I'd have lied to my teeth if he had. Ralph and I were so special. I knew I'd never find anyone who came close to being like him, not in a million years.'

The morning's rain had stopped. A fresh breeze blew into their faces as they walked up the hill towards the Heath, admiring the spacious green views over London. Beatrice had changed her lilac outfit for a simple cotton suit with a long jacket and slim-line skirt, and tied a silk scarf over her hair.

'This is such a special place, isn't it? In any weather and in every season it's like the Heath welcomes you to its heart.'

She flung an arm around Laura's shoulder.

'I'll always remember one very special evening in June 1903. I'd just turned twenty-one. Ralph and I had been to a party in The Bishops Avenue. It was midnight and we'd taken a cab back to Elm Row. Ralph suddenly asked the cab to stop and told him we'd walk the rest of the way. It was the most beautiful night: warm, balmy, with an enormous moon. We stood here on this very spot and Ralph asked me to marry him.'

'And he came dancing into the breakfast room in Chelsea the following morning,' Laura said. 'He was positively shimmering with joy. "She said yes!" he told me. He took me in his arms and we danced around the table together. I didn't need to ask him what he was talking about.'

'At least we can both remember him without bursting into tears.' She hugged Laura and then stiffened as a couple burst past them. A girl with long chestnut curls and a deep pink dress was being chased by a tall man in an expensive suit and hat. They were both choking with laughter.

'Good God!'

'What is it, Bea?'

She stared as the couple galloped across the Heath together, holding hands, and vanished into the cluster of trees.

'That man there, with the young girl. It's Harry Stallworthy, I'm sure of it. He's Miriam's husband … What on *earth* is he doing with a girl who looks young enough to be his daughter?'

Alexander

For the rest of February and well into March, Alexander took refuge in Sylvia's nursery.

He stripped her bed and put fresh sheets on it. He covered it with the patchwork quilt Lillian had painstakingly made for her, which Sylvia loved. He tidied her toys but he didn't pack them into their baskets. Her clothes hung neatly in the closet, exactly as they'd been on that devastating Thanksgiving night. Her little shoes and slippers stood in a line on the floor. Some strong denial-ridden thread in his heart refused to believe he'd never see his daughter again. He wanted to keep the room in every detail, just as she'd known it, ready for her return.

One afternoon at the end of February, which should have been Sylvia's third birthday, he walked into Macy's and bought her a china doll. He called her Mattie. She had a round face with heavily rouged cheeks, a pouting scarlet mouth, black hair parted into two thick plaits, and a long-skirted cream taffeta suit with gold braiding down the jacket.

He perched Mattie against a pillow on the patchwork quilt, touched her cold cheek and finally burst into floods of tears.

'In the deepest grief there is no weeping.'

He proved that wasn't always true. He'd never have believed he had so many tears waiting to gush out of his eyes from his heart.

He fell into a new routine.

He slept most of the morning in the single bed in the spare room, staggered to his feet around eleven o'clock and took a bath. He drank a gallon of sweet black coffee, and spent all afternoon walking the city: anywhere, everywhere, it hardly mattered, as long as he was on the move. That was the only time his grief softened and those bitter black memories, loaded with remorse, blunted their cruel knives.

When the skies began to darken he'd meander back to Greenwich Village. He chomped dutifully through an early evening meal in a cheap café, bought a bottle of whisky – never in the same place too often, in case the shopkeepers got to recognise him, started a dialogue, asked him personal questions – and returned to the house.

Then he'd take a glass and the bottle up to the nursery and sit on the floor, drinking slowly and steadily until his head swam, his hands shook, his eyes no longer focused – and the bottle was empty. When he was deep in his cups, he'd sing Sylvia her favourite lullabies, always in the same order and always out of tune.

He knew the shape, size and position of every toy. Tommy the teddy bear was an excellent drinking companion. Prim little Mattie was deeply shocked by his behaviour. Maureen and Amanda, Sylvia's other dolls, also disapproved. Coco the clown reckoned he was most entertaining, with a glorious sense of fun. William, the white wooden rocking horse, offered to gallop him away to a faraway land. But there was no escape. The tin motor bus had passengers sprawling from its roof and would be dangerous to hail. The palace coach was packed to its rafters. The milk van was empty: in it he might stow away without anyone knowing, but only until the milkman needed to fill it up. The tiger in Humpty Dumpty's circus ring wanted to eat him alive. The elephants and donkeys invited him to join them. He told them with regret he was destined for higher things.

He had no idea what these were. Sooner or later, he'd have to return to St Luke's. The hospital board were retaining him on half pay. Which was good of them. Half was better than nothing. He only had himself to feed and water but those demands still squeaked through the door. They lay piled on the dusty table, unpaid.

Any day now the hospital's compassion would end. They'd sack him. Call yourself a doctor? Nearly chopped somebody in two. What about *our* reputation? Sure, we covered for you, got someone else to perform surgery. Once is more than enough, old fruit. Got guys lined up around the block, wanting to do your job. Who the hell do you think you are?

He couldn't afford to live without his salary, he had no savings. He'd worked his way through medical school, swotted like crazy, beavered through the nights to pass those exams. And look at him now. Chucking years of hope and dreams and such sweet triumph down the drain.

Liquor didn't come cheap, not in the quantities he slugged daily down his throat.

The only people who might have helped were Lillian's parents. He lived in their house, so they could easily kick him out. One letter, one polite request, get stuffed, bye-bye pudding-faced baboon. He could hardly ask *them* for help.

And not a single word from Lillian. After three years of marriage and a daughter together she'd vanished in a three-minute farewell. Nice knowing you, buster. Got a rich Daddy, I have, so who needs *you*?

He still hadn't a clue where she was in Europe. I mean, don't they have pens and postcards in posh hotels? Can't people buy postage stamps when they need to?

Anyway, he was much too proud to ask for help. He'd got himself into this ghastly mess – and he was the only person who could dig himself out.

But he put off facing reality. Could he survive without the vast quantities of liquor he pumped daily into his veins? He didn't know because he was too scared to even try.

Then things changed. Oh yes, siree. Think you can't get any deeper into the black hole of Calcutta? Wanna bet? Well, lemme tell ya this, man. Slurp.

Suddenly, out of the blue, everything got one hell of a whole lot worse.

Saturday March 25th 1911 was a particularly mild day with a hint of spring. The trees in Central Park had just begun to reveal their delicate green foliage. He walked more slowly than usual, savouring the freshness of the air, noticing the world about him in more detail than he had during those agonising deep-winter months.

Maybe there was hope for him yet? Maybe he could stop drinking, get his act together and resume his role as a respected, hard-working doctor?

Yes, he would. Tomorrow. Right on, man. Make mine tomorrow. New leaf. Out of bed, fresh as a daisy. Empty every bottle down the drain. Clean the house, pay bills, climb on subway and say hi to Len.

Tomorrow.

The phone was ringing when he got back to the house. Usually he didn't bother to answer it, like he never opened the front door when anybody knocked or jangled the bell. Sometimes he shouted through the door for them to clear off and not come back. Mostly he ignored them. Whoever it was eventually gave up.

But that evening, the phone didn't stop. It rang every ten minutes. After an hour the infernal sound of it got the better of him. He crashed out of the nursery and downstairs to the hall. He felt like ripping the wire from its socket, but instead he took a deep breath and picked up the receiver.

It was Len.

'Alex, is that you? Hi, there! … How *are* you? … Good, good … Splendid … *Excellent* news.

'Listen, I'm sorry to disturb you at home, but we wanted you to know. There's been the most terrible accident. A fire at the Triangle Shirtwaist Factory. Catastrophic. It's in a block of flats west of Washington Square. The company employed five hundred teenage girls. *Teenagers, man.*

'Some of them were only fourteen years old.

'Just before five o'clock this afternoon, somebody must have dropped a match into a pile of fabric. Within minutes there was an inferno. The girls tried to escape but the doors had been locked from the inside. The fire spread from the eighth floor to the ninth. Many of the girls jumped from the windows. More than a hundred are dead.

'It's desperately ironic. They'd been fighting for safer working conditions for months but nobody listened. Now *this* has happened. Someone's going to have to carry the can, big time. Meanwhile, we have to cope with the injured and the dying. We need your help.

'Could you possibly come into St Luke's as soon as possible? It's all hands on deck here and we're desperate for your help.'

Stumbling over the words, hoping he'd subdued the drunken wobble in his voice, he said he'd be with Len in an hour. Len sounded so relieved. He practically sobbed with gratitude. Then he heard someone calling Len's name and the line went dead.

He put down the receiver and stared at the photograph on the wall above the phone. He and Lillian had posed for the camera, holding a two-day-old Sylvia in their arms. He'd forgotten how beautiful Lillian was. Those dark eyebrows, the shining hair, that enchanting smile. Her triumph and delight at becoming a mother. His own amazement and joy flooded back to him. It had been a million miserable years since he'd felt like that.

He'd received a bedraggled postcard from her. Saying how sorry she was but she had to leave him before she killed herself. She'd be back but she didn't know when. If only they hadn't given that party, she'd never have caught the virus … And now her father wasn't very well … They were still in Paris, by the way. The Louvre …

He pulled on a sweater and a pair of sneakers. He knew he was too drunk to go straight to St Luke's, but he felt a surge of relief that Len had even thought of ringing him. He'd never have done so without first consulting the other doctors. They wanted him back in their very special fold. They were willing to forgive and forget.

Maybe if he walked for half an hour, he could sober up.

He made some black coffee, heaped sugar into it and gulped it down.

Then he walked in what he hoped was a straight line through Greenwich Village to Washington Square.

Hundreds of other people were doing the same. Or rather, they were running in panic, pushing through the crowds, tripping over each other in their haste, trying to find their loved ones.

He reached the building and gawped at the chaos and carnage. The air was black with soot and dirt. Lumps of grime settled on his lips. He spat them off. Floods of water from the firemen's hoses, stained with blood, gushed into the gutters and slashed across his sneakers. People screamed, wept, fainted, dropped like flies, clutched at one another, hysterical with grief.

Frozen with fear, he stood and stared, his heart thumping, his legs like pulp.

Then he turned away and began to run.

The horrors of that night when he'd found Sylvia dead and Lillian dying came swarming back. There was no way he could do anything to help. Dealing with charred bodies, coping with the smell of burned hair and scorched clothes, the weeping relatives, joining forces with the other doctors and nurses? The very thought made him feel so nauseous he had to stop in his tracks.

He threw up on the sidewalk.

As he stood there, bent over his knees, wiping his mouth and trying to get his breath, he heard a voice behind him: soft, insidious, with an Irish lilt.

'Hi there, man … Wanna take something wonderful to help with your distress? … This acts real fast. Pure as the driven snow it is and no mistake. As close as you'll ever get to heaven on this scorched earth.'

∞

He lurched away from the voice and started to run. He didn't know for sure what he was being offered, but he could guess – and it got him thinking. Ever since that night when he had found nothing in their bathroom to help Lillian, he'd kept a black bag stuffed with emergency aid in the cupboard underneath the stairs. Tonight, finishing his bottle of whisky would never do the trick.

He got home, locked himself in and took the phone off the hook. He dug out the black bag. In it he found a bottle of morphine. Without bothering to read the instructions, he took a hefty dose. Then he finished the whisky. An hour later he was on such a high that he danced up and down the stairs, into every room, all over the house.

He finally collapsed on the first-floor landing, where he woke in the morning, his limbs frozen, his clothes stained with blood, his hands black with soot and the taste of vomit clogging up his tongue.

During the next few days he finished the morphine. He staggered out and raided six pharmacies within walking distance, buying every bottle of cough medicine he was allowed.

Not only were they perfectly legal, they also contained heroin. He had no appetite and often couldn't sleep. But he carried on drinking. Liquor and cough medicine. A swell remedy for pretty much everything you could name. If he wasn't high as a kite, he was sprawled out on the floor, dead to the world.

Exactly what he wanted.

One morning in the middle of April, it might have been a Saturday – he'd pretty much lost track of time – somebody started banging on his front door.

He was still slopping around the house in his pyjamas, unshaven, unwashed and bleary-eyed. He tried to ignore the noise, but the banging continued. Then the intruder started hanging on the doorbell like there was no tomorrow.

He limped into the hall.

'Whoever you are,' he yelled, 'go away and leave me alone!'

'Al? … Alexander, is that you? … Open the *door*, for God's sake … It's me, Theo … I've come all the way from London, so will you kindly let me in.'

He reeled with shock. He clung on to the nearest piece of furniture to keep himself from falling. He opened his mouth to say Hi! only to discover he was mute.

'Come on, little brother … I've travelled halfway round the world specially to see you … Open this door before I kick it down!'

He didn't have much choice. He could hardly leave his own *brother* standing on the doorstep. He unlocked the door, opened it and caught his breath. Theo looked so handsome standing there, so suave, groomed and well-dressed, sparkling like a diamond with the sun behind him.

Theo said, 'Jesus *Christ*, Alexander … Just *look* at the state of you!'

'I'm sorry.' He pulled at his pyjama jacket. He wasn't even wearing a bath robe. He felt pathetic and filthy – and utterly humiliated.

Theo took him in his arms. 'You've lost a load of weight, Alexander Hertzler. And you stink to high heaven and beyond.'

'I'm sorry, Theo … What must you think of me? I was just going to – '

Theo closed the front door and turned to face him. 'Where's Lillian? Where the *hell* is that wife of yours? How come she's let you get into such a state?'

'She's just gone to the shops,' he muttered. 'She'll be back any minute.'

'And you expect me to believe you?' Theo glanced at the muddy footprints down the hall, the dusty table, the telephone receiver lying off its hook. 'She's left you, hasn't she? ... I must say, given the state you're in, I'm not surprised.' He moved towards him and opened his eyes wide with his fingers. 'Hmm ... Not only liquor, I see ... What *else* have you been taking?'

Silently, Alex pulled away.

'Are you out of your *mind*, Al? The stuff will kill you if you go on like this. Nobody will ever employ you again. What are you trying to do? Self-destruct?'

'You haven't a clue what it's been like.'

'I can guess, and you've got to snap out of it. Right now. This very minute.' Theo took his hand and led him up the stairs. 'I'll run you a bath ... I assume there's hot water. The house is freezing. Do you have any clean clothes?'

He nodded like an obedient child. 'In a drawer somewhere.'

'Thank God for small mercies. When you're washed and dressed, I'll take you to the barber. He can whip that beard off and cut your hair. Then we'll have the best breakfast New York has to offer ... When did you last eat a decent meal?'

'I can't remember.' At the thought of food, his stomach churned.

'Rare steak,' Theo announced with gusto. 'That's what you need. Eggs sunny-side-up, strong coffee, hot rolls glistening with butter. But I'm not eating a single mouthful sitting opposite a chimpanzee.'

He mumbled, 'How did you know?'

'One of your doctor friends wrote to me ... Leonard

44

Grant … Said he'd been trying to get in touch with you for weeks. Lovely letter, nice guy … You'd promised to help at St Luke's after that fire but you never turned up. It got me so worried I thought I'd better come to see you. So I put my ailing ladies on hold and sailed the high seas. I've only got one brother. My ladies can wait. You obviously cannot.'

Alexander choked with self-pity. 'It's real good of you to care.'

Theo marched into the bathroom and turned on the taps.

'Oh, this is just the beginning, dearest bro. I'm not leaving you to rot in this house with those disgusting bottles. The place smells like a brewery. When you've cleaned up your act and dried out, I'm hauling you off with me to England.'

He gaped. 'I can't leave everything at the drop of a hat!'

'Oh yes, you can, easy as apple pie.' Theo straightened his back. Steam billowed around him. He gave him a long hard stare. 'I won't listen to *any* pathetic excuses. You can come off the liquor *and* the drugs and start to live your life again as a decent human being.'

He opened his mouth to say he was *trying* to stay alive the only way he knew. Instead, tears began to pour down his cheeks.

Theo put his hands on his hips.

'I'm not taking no for an answer. Now, strip off those filthy rags and climb into this lovely hot tub.' He turned at the doorway. 'And while you're scrubbing up, I'm going to search this house for bottles. I shall pour every last drop of alcohol and God in heaven only knows *what* else you've been drinking down the plughole.'

Alexander waited until Theo had shut the door. He peeled off his pyjamas and threw them into the trash can. He could hardly bear the stench of his own body. Gingerly, he

45

climbed into the tub. He let the water stream over him. He tipped back his head. The water pulled at his hair. He lay there staring at the ceiling, desperate for a drink.

England's green and pleasant land can go to hell. All I want to do right now is to drown.

Beatrice

'That was delicious.' Victor dabbed his serviette to his mouth in a fastidious gesture she'd seen so many times before. They were dining alone together in St John's Wood at the end of June. 'My compliments to Mrs Browning.'

'I'm glad you enjoyed our supper.'

'By the way.' Victor shifted his chair away from the table, tactfully waiting until their butler had disappeared with the dishes and closed the door. 'I've been meaning to ask you … How's that sister of yours?'

'Miriam?' Beatrice hastily drank the last of her wine, feeling it sear her throat. 'I haven't seen her for weeks. Laura and I have been so busy. Funnily enough, I've just finished making Charlotte a new summer frock for her best friend's birthday party. I must take it over to her.' She looked across at Victor, dreading to hear his news. 'Why do you ask?'

'There's been talk in the clubs about Harry.'

'Oh?' She tried to sound surprised. 'What have people been saying?'

'I had luncheon with Sir Antony Westport yesterday. He's

one of our bank's most important clients. He says Harry has been seen gallivanting around London, bold as brass, with a gorgeous young redhead.' Victor folded his serviette into a neat rectangle and poured himself a brandy. 'I mean, *very* young. That's hardly a description of Miriam, is it?'

'No.' She took a deep breath. She'd no intention of telling Victor she'd already seen the redhead and had desperately hoped that in the intervening weeks Harry might have stopped romping around with her. 'No, it certainly isn't.'

'Could you find out what's going on, Beatrice? We wouldn't want any scandal to taint our family, would we now?'

'Of course not, Victor. I'll take tea with Miriam tomorrow. I'll drop in without letting her know beforehand, so she won't be able to plan anything. I'm sure Harry will be there as usual.'

'Let's hope so. Their marriage has always seemed watertight, but you never can tell. Harry has so much money he's never had to work for a living. Chaps with a lot of time on their hands can often go astray if they're not encouraged to toe the line.'

Remembering how Harry had clung on to the hand of the gorgeous redhead as they vanished together into the trees on Hampstead Heath, Beatrice smothered a laugh. Toeing the line? Harry had obviously crossed it, lock stock and barrel, several months ago. She needed to change the subject, and fast.

She stood up and moved towards her husband. 'Finish your brandy, darling.' She ran her fingers through his thick dark hair, touched with the first threads of silver. 'What would you say to an early night?'

Victor grinned up at her. 'I'd say that would be a most delicious end to a delicious evening.'

⌒

She ordered a cab the following afternoon to take her to Kensington.

'You'll have to spare me for a few hours,' she told Laura. 'Victor has heard on the grapevine that something's up with Harry. I need to talk to Miriam, find out what's going on … I'll take the dress we made for Charlotte. Can we find something really beautiful that'll fit Miriam? It might be a clever way to start an intimate and possibly difficult conversation.'

'Of course.' Laura bustled along the racks of dresses, pulling out several long chiffon frocks and holding them up for inspection. 'Will one of these do?'

'The emerald green is perfect. Ask one of the girls to wrap it for me.'

'Good luck, darling … This might all be a storm in a teacup, so keep smiling through.'

As the cab trundled across London, she suddenly remembered an argument she'd had with Miriam, as fresh and painful in her memory as if it were yesterday. She was seven years old. She wanted the seventeen-year-old Miriam to take her for a walk on the Heath. Miriam snapped at her, told her she was too busy. When she'd protested that her sister had nothing to do but enjoy herself and could easily spare her half an hour, Miriam had rounded on her, her dark hair flying, her eyes spitting venom.

'If it weren't for you,' Miriam hissed, 'our mother would still be alive. Having you, the agony of it, killed her. *How I wish you'd never been born.*'

The sisters avoided each other for weeks afterwards. Miriam's resentment would always come between them.

∞

In many ways she envied her sister. Miriam had met Harry Stallworthy at a dance when she was seventeen. She remained besotted from that evening on. She floated over the surface of life like a beautiful lily in a weed-free lake on which sunlight always shone.

She and Harry were the ideal couple. They laughed at the same jokes, danced the same crazy modern dances, drank pungent American cocktails, shared a small circle of exclusive friends, took long foreign holidays and never bothered to count the cost of anything. Harry, who had inherited a vast family fortune, had never done a day's work in his life. His younger brother, Jonathan, travelled to India to work in the Diplomatic Service and only came home every eight years on a flying visit.

Nasty things never happened to Harry and Miriam. Other people had coughs, colds and influenza. Miriam was never ill. Other couples struggled with money worries. Harry's bottomless purse solved every problem. Other women worried about their staff and their workloads; not having the vote; needing to deal with alcoholic husbands, elderly parents and sick children; the sheer difficulty of managing the complications of ordinary life.

Miriam couldn't have cared less about politics, the stock market or women's rights. She had servants to handle every domestic problem. Her pregnancies had been trouble-free; the births of Charlotte and the twins casebook perfect. She retained her trim figure, clear complexion, luxuriant hair and ready laugh. Often, when Beatrice saw Miriam's light-hearted, carefree way with her children, her envy darkened into a fierce jealousy.

In her most painful moments she told herself that *nobody's* life could be so trouble-free. Sooner or later, Miriam would find herself in a tunnel filled with problems she didn't know how to handle because apart from their mother's death, and much later their father's, she'd had no experience of pain.

But that particular June afternoon, the moment she saw Miriam sitting alone in her Kensington garden under the willow tree, her unusual stillness warned her something was wrong.

Miriam spotted her sister walking across the lawn and held out her hand. It was cool to the touch, her cheek damp as she bent to kiss it.

'Beatrice … How lovely … I'm afraid I'm on my own. Charlotte's playing tennis with Rosalind. The boys are with Foxie, splashing about in a boat on the Serpentine. I don't expect any of them until six. And Harry is … Harry's in Yorkshire.'

'No matter. It's you I've come to see.' She held out her parcels. 'Two beautiful new frocks, one for you, one for Charlotte.'

'How incredibly kind of you.' Miriam's eyes sparked with sudden tears. 'I'll open them with her tonight. She'll be thrilled.'

She pulled a chair closer and settled into it. 'Please tell me what's wrong?'

'Nothing whatsoever, sister dear!' Miriam avoided her eyes, waving an arm at a hovering butler. 'Could we have some tea, please, Williams? Cucumber sandwiches, scones, lots of cake. Ginger and that lovely lemon drizzle.'

'You can't pull the wool like that.' She took a deep breath and persevered. 'Is Harry thriving?'

'I don't want to talk about him.'

'So something *is* wrong.'

'Nothing I can solve or manage … Not this time.'

'What do you mean?'

Miriam bit her lip. 'The same old story, I'm afraid.'

'*What* story. You and Harry are the perfect couple – '

'We may put up the perfect front, but Harry's always had an eye for other women.'

'I had no idea. You never told me.'

'Why should I? It's not something you blab about. Over the years, I've accepted it. It never lasts long. He has brief flings, always with younger women. I know exactly when they start – and in the past, I've managed to survive them.' Tears stood on Miriam's cheeks. 'I wait until the first flush of passion has died and then I use every trick in the book to win him back.' She fiddled with a damp curl clinging to her neck. 'But this time, it's different.'

'*How* different?'

'Harry's utterly bewitched. He's mad with lust … With love … Call it what you will. The first flush, instead of dying, has become an inferno.'

'Who on earth is he in love with?'

Miriam flinched. 'An "actress" called Dora Peberdy. Oh, she doesn't do Shakespeare or anything grand. Only music-hall rubbish. The girl thinks she can sing. She can't, of course. She warbles like a cat on heat. She's got masses of flaming red hair and she's eighteen years old.'

'But Harry's forty-two … Old enough to be – '

'Her father … Exactly … I've never met her or seen her, but a friend of mine has told me more than enough. Harry doesn't care who knows how he feels … I'm at my wits' end, Beatrice. I don't know what to do.'

Williams brought the tea-tray. For a few minutes the sisters were silent. As the butler walked back to the house, Miriam murmured, 'My hands are tied, of course. I've a little money of my own but not enough to last me the rest of my life. Certainly not enough to support the children.

We're sending the twins to Eton in the autumn – we've had their names down since the day they were born. I don't see why Harry's disgusting behaviour should jeopardise their education.

'Charlotte wants to be presented at Court next summer. Eton and the Buck House party season will cost a fortune. I've always been a faultless wife and divorce is not on the cards. So I can only watch and wait – and pray!'

Beatrice accepted her cup of tea, her mouth parched. 'Do the children know what's going on?'

Miriam swallowed half a scone, heaped with raspberry jam.

'The twins are completely innocent and unaware. I only hope they stay that way. Charlotte has asked me several times where her father is. I've told her he has business in the City. I'll invent some problem that's taken him to Yorkshire, to cover longer absences.'

'Where's Harry now?'

'With Dora, of course.' Miriam's cup rattled in its saucer. 'He's bought her a flat in Bloomsbury – '

'Good *God*, Miriam!'

'Shocking, isn't it?' Miriam cut a hefty slice of ginger cake. 'But it's better than being seen with her all over London where the gossips can salivate and the photographers click their cameras.' She attacked a second slice. 'As long as the affair stays out of the newspapers I'll be grateful for small mercies.'

Beatrice declined the last scone and gulped her tea, almost afraid to ask. 'Do you still ...' She faltered.

'Share the same bed?' Miriam's eyes burned with fury. 'Certainly not! I'm getting my own back the only way I can.'

'I hope you don't mean – '

'That I've taken a lover?' Miriam lowered her voice. 'As

a matter of fact, I have. It's the first time I've ever been to bed with another man, but I really don't see why Harry should have everything his way.'

She stared at her sister, feeling as if she were looking at a stranger. 'So who *is* this lover of yours?'

'A Frenchman, Emile Dubois. You may have heard of him. He's a brilliant novelist. His work has just been translated into English. His novels are wonderful sagas about family life, full of passion and contemporary detail. He gave a reading last month for a small gathering of invited guests. He has a wonderfully seductive speaking voice. I could have listened to him all day and all night, not just for an hour.

'Afterwards there were drinks. I was introduced and we started chatting. He was enchanting. He asked me to have luncheon with him. I thought, why the hell not?' Miriam flushed. 'Emile's a very attractive man. He says all the right things in a wonderfully French way. After being totally ignored by Harry for three months, it was bliss. I drank a great deal of champagne in Emile's hotel suite and found myself in bed with him.' She smiled to herself. 'It was absolutely glorious.'

'For heaven's *sake*, Miriam.' Beatrice put down her empty cup, thirstier than ever. 'You do realise you're playing with fire!'

'No, I'm not. I know exactly what I'm doing. Having a marvellous summer fling. At the end of July, when Emile's publicity tour closes, we'll say farewell. He'll go home to Saint-Tropez. I'll take the children to Scotland.'

'With Harry?'

'At the moment,' Miriam's almond eyes shone dark with pain, 'I neither know nor care. If I had a choice, I'd probably take Emile.'

∞

Miserably, the sisters finished their tea. Beatrice was starving but couldn't eat a thing. She wondered how much she'd have the courage to tell Victor.

'Enough of my problems.' Miriam made an effort to talk about somebody else. 'How are *you*, Beatrice? Any babies on the way?'

'Not yet.' She told Miriam about Theo's advice.

'You'd be crazy to listen to him. If you leave your enterprise, Laura will find another designer. And if you leave Victor on his own in London, heaven only knows what he'll get up to. You'll be asking for trouble.'

She said primly, 'My husband would *never* cheat on me!'

'How can you be so sure?'

'He's not a bit like Harry. For a start, he has a full-time job. You know how stuffy and correct his bank is. He'd never risk even a hint of scandal. He's not a flirt. I trust him completely.'

'Victor's not a saint, Beatrice. He's flesh and blood.'

'But I'm desperate to have a child. What's the point in consulting a top gynaecologist if I don't take his advice?'

Miriam shrugged. 'It's your life.' For a fleeting moment she looked old and haggard. 'But if the worst happens, don't say you haven't been warned.'

Charlotte

In the middle of that July 1910 in London, it started to rain. It poured steadily, night and day, for an entire week. The sound of the rain hammered on window panes. Puddles swirled over garden paths and flooded the streets. Drains gurgled and clogged. Dark grey clouds raced across the sky. Birds screeched and squabbled on window sills, flapping drenched feathers.

The Stallworthys' large house in Kensington bore the brunt of the weather with stolid fortitude. In its time, it had seen much worse. Charlotte and the twins, Blair and Russell, and Foxie their governess, had the spacious fourth floor to themselves, but even so, the noise the twins made bounced off the ceilings and echoed throughout the house.

Blair loved nothing more than rushing around their garden or across one of the London parks. Shutting him indoors was like caging a lion cub. He picked fights with his brother that involved pillows and a great deal of shouting and rolling around on the floor. Russell couldn't keep up with him physically, but he read more fluently and he was more interested in arguing and finding out the meaning of words.

Charlotte was desperate to play tennis with Rosalind, who often had a handsome tennis coach in tow; to gossip with her best friend over tea, or help Foxie with some light shopping in Kensington. But the vile weather called a halt to everything.

By Friday their mother had had enough. Miriam snapped at everyone, even Foxie, who could usually do no wrong. They were ordered out of the house.

'Take those infernal children off my hands, Foxie,' Miriam said. She stuffed another chocolate into her plump mouth. 'The twins are giving me a thumping headache. Go somewhere educational this morning and then take them to luncheon. Give them something healthy but substantial to eat and make sure they clear their plates. I'll be out this afternoon and I don't want to see any of them until tomorrow. If it rains again and they get wet along the way, give them a hot bath when you get back.' She added sotto voce, but nobody heard: 'And preferably drown them in the process.'

She slammed her bedroom door. The house rocked.

Foxie lined up the children in the hall. She inspected their hats, their summer coats, their shining faces, clean teeth, immaculate fingernails and polished shoes. Then she marched them out the door.

'We're off to the British Museum. There's always such a wonderful lot to see there. Fossils, rocks, pots, statues … Come on, now, spit spot.'

They climbed on to the omnibus to Bloomsbury. Charlotte longed to be with Rosalind, wearing her cream linen tennis dress with its gracefully flared skirt, learning to serve, throwing the ball high into a clear blue sky, thwacking at it as it spun to land.

The bus was damp, crowded and uncomfortable. It stank of sweaty bodies. The twins began to point and giggle at a woman's hat immediately in front of them. Its decoration of artificial cherries bounced up and down with the jolts of the bus. Blair reached out a hand to pull one off.

Foxie dug him in the ribs. 'Don't you dare,' she hissed.

That made everything worse. The twins' gasps of hysterical laughter encouraged heads to turn and curious eyes to stare.

Once they'd reached their stop, Foxie insisted that Blair and Russell walk either side of her to keep them apart. She followed in their wake. Foxie was slim and small-boned. The twins had shot up since January and were almost as tall as she was. The rain had stopped and a weak sun struggled through the clouds, but huge muddy puddles shone everywhere. Blair asked if he could jump in one. Foxie threatened to put him in a cab and send him home in disgrace. Russell chortled, Blair grinned.

They walked down a short bit of Oxford Street and crossed a noisy Tottenham Court Road, dodging the splattering of horses' hooves and lurching carriages. They were in Russell Street, very near the British Museum, when Charlotte glanced across the road.

Which is when she saw a very familiar figure.

Her father.

In that first moment she could hardly believe her eyes.

None of them had seen hide nor hair of Father for more than a fortnight. Mother told her he'd travelled up to Yorkshire to look after one of his houses. There had been problems with the land surrounding it and the nearby lake, Mother said vaguely, obviously making up the story as she went along. A dispute that needed his particular attention.

He'd be back as soon as he could leave the matter in the hands of his caretaker.

Charlotte almost grabbed Foxie's shoulder to ask her to stop. She wanted to wave an arm to Father, shout across the road, dodge the lethal carriages and snorting horses, and race into his arms.

But something made her hesitate.

Father carried an enormous bunch of bright flowers and several gaudily wrapped parcels. He walked briskly, jauntily, with purpose, as if he could hardly wait to reach his destination. He wore a crisp summer suit and a stylish hat, neither of which she'd ever seen before. He bowed gracefully, raising his hat to a woman who passed him, a sparkle in his eyes.

And in that instant she knew that neither the flowers nor the parcels were for Mother or for her or the twins. She shrank behind Foxie and her brothers, into their glimmering shadows, and looked the other way. Moments later, when she glanced behind her, Father had disappeared.

Inside, the British Museum was cool and dimly lit. Murmuring voices billowed from nowhere, echoing up to the vaulted ceilings and floating down again on giant cobwebs of sound. People in damp raincoats and muddy boots seemed out of place and insignificant, scurrying like busy ants among the grandeur of perfect pottery and gigantic, disdainful statues.

She trotted dutifully behind the twins, her head spinning with disbelief and a host of worried questions. Perhaps it hadn't been Father after all, but somebody who looked remarkably like him? If it *had* been him, perhaps the flowers and gifts *were* for Mother? She stared blindly at the priceless museum collections, meticulously arranged behind their spotless glass – and saw only Father's face, the flirtatious sparkle in his eyes, his hand reaching for his elegant hat.

She'd always adored her father. He had a ceaseless energy that set everyone alight. An excellent sportsman, he swam in the lake on holiday, rode his horse in Hyde Park, fenced with breath-taking speed and precision in a London Club, and was one of the best dancers she'd ever seen.

In their spacious living room, he'd taught her how to waltz, twirling her around in his arms, exquisitely light-footed, innately musical. When he wasn't at home, their house felt smaller, duller, more ordinary. Everybody waited on tenterhooks for his return.

Mother tried to keep up with him, but Charlotte knew that in the past few years, she hadn't always been successful, letting him go out alone to parties and dances, saying she felt too tired but promising, 'I'll come with you tomorrow.'

Those flowers, those parcels … She knew it *had* been Father holding them, dancing down the street, barely containing his impatience to arrive at his destination.

So where had he been going? And who were the gifts for?

'Charlotte!' Foxie grabbed her elbow. 'Please keep up with us and kindly concentrate! I've been telling the twins about these *spectacular* Roman coins. You obviously haven't listened to a single word.'

Miriam was out when they got home. Charlotte hung around the landing all evening, wanting to see her mother, longing to talk. She couldn't just ignore what she'd seen. She couldn't possibly tell the twins, nor did she want to talk about her father to Foxie.

She went to bed at ten o'clock but kept her door open. Around midnight she heard a carriage rattling down the street. It stopped outside their house. Voices twanged on the doorstep, then a key turned in the lock.

She slipped silently on to the landing, down a flight of stairs, leaning dangerously over the banister to listen.

A man's voice murmured, '*Au revoir, chérie!*'

Mother said, 'Goodnight, Emile, darling. Shall I see you tomorrow?'

'*Naturellement!… Jusqu'à demain, mon amour.*'

Then she was sure she heard them kiss.

The front door closed.

She shrank back into the shadows.

Her heart beating fit to burst, she raced silently upstairs, into her room.

Charlotte sat on her bed, her head buzzing with worries.

She thought the unthinkable. That her beloved father had left home and was living somewhere in London with another woman. That her mother was gadding about town with a Frenchman who kissed her goodnight and would see her tomorrow.

Was this what married life was all about? Living an enormous lie?

She felt angry and humiliated. Neither of her parents had bothered to talk to her, or told her what was happening. Surely she was old enough to be taken into their confidence? Had she stumbled on a terrible secret?

What should she do? Pretend she'd heard and seen nothing? Wait for something to happen? In her bones, she knew things would get even worse.

The following day, she watched her mother carefully. Miriam looked pale and tired. Charlotte failed to find the courage to ask if she could talk to her in private. After luncheon her mother disappeared 'to visit some friends'. It was on the tip of her tongue to say something to Foxie, but the rain blissfully stopped.

She was allowed to visit her friend Rosalind's house, two streets away. Skimming the tennis ball with relish over the net, laughing, gossiping about their friends, she persuaded herself that nothing was seriously wrong.

But next morning a sudden rustling panic seized their house. Very early, before breakfast, the telephone started to ring: once, twice, three times. Miriam dashed in and out of the hall in her dressing gown, holding a flurry of newspapers, summoning Foxie to her study, shutting the door. Voices rose and fell, muted but urgent. Auntie Bea arrived to join them. She stayed for half an hour. She left the house abruptly, slamming the front door.

Charlotte was truly astonished. Her beloved aunt had paid them a visit without coming up to see her and the twins? She'd wanted to thank her for the stunning new frock. She'd wear it for Rosalind's birthday party in two weeks' time.

She still didn't know what was going on – but now she'd filled with dread.

Then, that afternoon, came the bad news.

'We're going down to Cornwall,' Foxie said briskly, her mouth snapping like a toad swallowing a fly. 'Tomorrow morning, first thing. We're going to St Ives for the summer to stay in a lovely big hotel called Tregenna Castle … Now, I want you all to decide what to take. Start packing your bags.'

The twins, crowing with delight, bounced into their bedroom to fight over their favourite toys and dig out their buckets and spades.

Charlotte waited until they were out of earshot. Then she asked, deliberately innocent and childlike, 'When will Father be joining us, Foxie? I do so miss him.'

62

Foxie bustled across the room to open a trunk. She stuck her face in it, but she could see their governess had flushed a furious scarlet.

'He might join us later, Charlotte. When he's solved his problems in Yorkshire.'

She almost said, 'But he isn't in –'

Then she thought better of it.

She said, 'But why are we leaving so *soon*? It's only July … Rosalind has asked me to her party. She'll be *so* upset if I'm not there. And we're going to have six special tennis lessons together, with –'

'I'm sorry, Charlotte.' Foxie straightened her back. Her face had changed from scarlet to yellowish. 'You'll have to cancel your plans. You've got time to write some letters of apology if you start now. I've put a nice new pen on your desk for you.'

'But *why*? What's *happened*? What's the *rush* to get out of town?'

Foxie moved towards her and touched her shoulder. Her eyes glittered with a strange, sad sympathy.

'Ask me no questions, Charlotte, and you'll be told no lies.'

'Ask me no questions!' As if she were three years old and confined to the nursery. Or being pushed around Kensington Gardens by her nanny in a squeaky perambulator.

The twins were different. They were only twelve: silly little boys who couldn't see any further than their pillow fights or petty squabbles. Next spring she would be seventeen. A young woman! She'd be presented at Court. Old enough for parties and dancing … and even suitors. Mother had met Father when *she* was seventeen and fallen in love at first sight.

She lay in bed, wide awake, until midnight. Until she heard her mother close her bedroom door and the rest of the household was asleep.

She tiptoed downstairs into Miriam's study. She switched on the lamp above her desk. Papers littered every surface. The waste-paper basket overflowed with what looked like several drafts of the same letter.

She knew Miriam kept her diary in a bottom drawer of her desk, although she'd never dared to open and read it. Now she bent and scooped it out. She opened it at that day's date: Friday 22nd July 1910. Miriam had written a three-line entry, the inky letters blotched with tears.

I have sent Harry's solicitor an urgent letter. I have swallowed my pride. I have said all will be forgiven if Harry immediately comes to his senses. I have begged him to come home. I only hope things have not gone too far and it's not too late.

Stuffed between the pages was a folded newspaper cutting. Her legs shook as she smoothed it out. The feature, headed *The Distinctly Separate Lives of the Wealthy Stallworthys* included four photographs:

Father standing outside a Bond Street jewellers on the arm of a young woman dressed to the nines in a frilly frock and a ridiculous feathery hat.

The same young woman standing on a music-hall stage, a spotlight on her heavily made-up face.

Miriam in full evening dress leaving the Royal Opera House with a dark-haired man Charlotte had never seen before.

And a sepia photo of Mother and Father on their wedding day, glamorous and beautiful, cutting an enormous celebration cake. A crooked black line had been drawn down the middle, slashing them apart.

She couldn't be bothered to read the wretched article. She'd seen quite enough.

Miriam said not a word to her next morning except to ask whether she'd packed enough underwear and her prettiest summer frocks. She and Foxie kept up the pretence that nothing was wrong: all that day on the train to Cornwall, and when they reached Tregenna Castle, and the next day in the gardens and throughout their meals in the dining room, and the next day when they shopped in St Ives and walked along the beach.

A bright, smiling façade, though their smiles never reached their eyes and they whispered miserably to each other when they thought she wasn't looking.

'Father will soon be joining us,' Miriam said from time to time, pushing her hair behind her ears, adjusting her summer hat, smoothing her long soft skirt, touching the pearls at her throat with quivering fingers. And eating. Anything she could forage after breakfast and between all their meals. 'Any day now his business problems will be resolved … You'll see … He sends you his love, of course.'

But he so obviously wasn't sending them anything, let alone love, that she'd no idea why her mother even bothered to pretend. The only person she was trying to convince was herself. Father must have known where they were. He never telephoned, not once. He never even sent a postcard.

And how he'd have loved Tregenna Castle, a huge hotel at the top of a steep hill that overlooked St Ives. From its high windows she could see for miles: the coastline, the sea itself and its changing colours, the glorious scarlet sunsets, acres of wonderful sky that made her want to join the raucous gulls flying around it.

Father would have taken them running in the gardens,

overtaken the twins in a race skimming down the hill. He'd have joked with the waiters at mealtimes, filling the dining room with his mammoth laugh. He'd have brought their holiday to life.

She missed him so much her heart ached.

Tregenna Castle was full of families with fathers. Only the Stallworthys were bereft. She was so angry with Miriam for getting them into their dire situation, for accepting Father's absence for a single minute, let alone an entire summer, that she decided not to talk to her. She hoped by being sulky and silent, her mother would see how hurt she was. But Miriam hardly noticed. She didn't give a jot about her feelings. She might just as well not be there.

One day in August, two things happened.

A man with dark oily hair, a dapper moustache and a French accent 'introduced' himself to Miriam at Tregenna while they were having tea. Charlotte recognised him at once: the man in the newspaper photograph. He wore a beige linen suit and smelled of a sharp green-pine scent. When he bent over Miriam's hand and kissed it, his hair flopped on to his forehead like a spaniel's ears.

Miriam looked up at him, her face alight with joy. Then, rapidly, she pretended to be overwhelmed by surprise.

'Why, Monsieur Dubois!' Her voice trilled with happiness. 'What an *extraordinary* coincidence … I haven't seen you since your marvellous talk in London! I thought you were back on the Côte d'Azur.'

'*Mais non, Madame* … I have rooms at the Porthminster Hotel, just down the hill. It's not as grand as your Tregenna Castle but it – how you say? – serves my purpose. I'm truly delighted to see you again!'

'May I present my beautiful children and their formidable

governess? … Charlotte, this is the famous novelist, Monsieur Emile Dubois.'

This was the man who'd kissed her mother goodnight in London only weeks before. They must have arranged to meet at Tregenna. She despised Miriam even more for thinking she could deceive her family so easily.

Monsieur Dubois bent his head towards her.

'Mademoiselle … Je suis enchanté … Pas de Monsieur … I hope you will call me Uncle Emile.'

Her skin crawled.

That same evening a new family arrived at Tregenna.

'My word! I do believe that's Baroness Manners,' Miriam whispered excitedly, fingering her pearls with one hand while picking out another chocolate with the other. 'Isn't she glamorous? Her husband's an important man in the government: at the Prime Minister's right hand, people say, the real power behind the throne. I've *always* wanted to meet them.'

But Charlotte only had eyes for their son. When he walked into the dining room, she could see him looking at her over everyone's heads. Tall, with ash-blond hair and sparkling light-blue eyes that shone into hers. She stared at him across the tables.

He and his family ate quickly and left the dining room before they did, but from that moment she watched out for him. She heard his mother call him Sebastian. The most romantic name in the world. She whispered it into her pillow every night.

Of course the situation was hopeless. Neither of them was ever without their family. Sebastian was always accompanied by two younger sisters and often by his parents. She was interminably surrounded by Foxie and the twins.

Every now and then she and Sebastian smiled secretly at each other if they happened to pass in the corridor. One morning, coming down to breakfast, their shoulders brushed on the stairs. She almost stumbled and fell down the entire flight with the thrill of his touch.

In a spin of excitement, Miriam sent Baroness Manners an invitation to tea. The Baroness made a pathetic excuse and declined. Furious and humiliated, Miriam took it as a giant snub. Charlotte knew that if her father had been with them, the Manners' family would have accepted with alacrity.

The fact that Uncle Emile now ate dinner with them every evening at Tregenna certainly didn't help. Foxie insisted they all speak French throughout the meal.

'This is a unique opportunity to improve your accents. Now we have the distinguished Monsieur Dubois at our table. A modern novelist of considerable and growing reputation, both here and abroad. Have you ever read ... '

That didn't help either. She sat red-faced with embarrassment as the twins clumsily translated the menu into appalling French and then dissolved into helpless giggles, hanging off their chairs and stuffing serviettes into their mouths. How could she ever hope to be sophisticated and stylish with *them* around?

She began to despair. She and Sebastian would never find an opportunity to meet and talk. She daydreamed of an assignation under the pine trees in Tregenna's gardens; of walking down the hill into St Ives, past the narrow river and its gushing waterfall; of holding his hand, standing on tiptoe to kiss his mouth.

The more daring her daydreams, the harsher their reality froze, the wider the gap between them grew. September cantered towards them. Soon they might be separated for ever.

On the morning of the twins' thirteenth birthday, she woke to find an envelope pushed underneath her door. She scrabbled to open it. Inside lay a small white card with firm black handwriting.

'I think you are wonderful,' it said. It was signed *'SM'*.

She blushed with surprise and delight. She longed to reply. *'Meet me tonight in the gardens by the river. CS.'* But she didn't dare.

She hid the card in her pocket. Tregenna's chef made them a special birthday picnic to eat on the beach. The twins built a massive sandcastle and played cricket with Uncle Emile. He'd bought them a kite for their birthday. Together, as Miriam watched, laughing encouragement, they flew it into the wind, shrieking with delight. The sun shone, the gulls swooped, the sand nuzzled hot and smooth between her toes.

Tomorrow was Saturday. Tomorrow night, Tregenna would host a dance at the hotel. Miriam said she could go. She'd wear her beautiful new frock, intended for Rosalind's birthday party. It hung in her wardrobe at the hotel, pale pink, with frills at the hem, short sleeves to show off her slim arms, and a neck as low as any she'd ever worn.

She could hardly wait to put it on – and make sure Sebastian noticed how pretty she looked in it. She intended to dance with him, even if she had to ask him herself. She'd float across the dance floor in his arms. The whole world would see them together.

She smiled at her stupid fat mother for the first time in weeks, wondering whether Sebastian had any idea what she planned for him.

But she didn't wonder for long.

Next day, her frothy little house of hopes and dreams came crashing around her ears. Miriam woke her at the crack of dawn. She beckoned her into her room. Through clenched teeth she said there'd been a terrible accident in the Lake District.

Father had been killed.

Charlotte gasped with disbelief. The questions spilled out of her.

'How? Where was he? What happened? Who found him?'

But Miriam, white-faced, tear-stained, held up her hand for silence.

'I don't know all the details, Charlotte. I'm devastated and terribly sorry. I must go home at once to organise the funeral. I'll leave you in Foxie's capable hands.' A sob choked her. 'I insist you be on your best behaviour. Set the twins a good example.' She looked her in the eyes. 'I know these past few weeks without your father haven't been easy – '

She longed to blurt out, 'I saw him. That day we went to the British Museum,' but she suddenly realised that was the last time she'd *ever* see her father. Tears welled up: stinging, burning, blinding.

'And I'm sorry,' Miriam added, 'if lately I've been distant and preoccupied. Now, would you be a dear sweet girl? Ask the twins to come in. I must talk to them.'

An hour later, accompanied by the hastily summoned, immaculately oiled and perfumed Emile Dubois and several suitcases, Miriam left for the London train.

Silently, Foxie packed their clothes. She'd been crying: her face was mottled and blotchy. Charlotte felt sorry for her – but even more sorry for herself. Every time she blinked, an image of Father blurred before her eyes: roaring with laughter at a family joke, waving his elegant hat, racing the twins down a hill, dancing to the gramophone.

'Why do we have to leave Tregenna?' she asked Foxie. 'Where are we *going*?'

This time Foxie gave her a straight answer.

'It would be *totally* disrespectful to your dear father for us to remain on holiday and pretend nothing's happened. We'll stay with your Aunt Beatrice and Uncle Victor at Chandos Manor. Your mother spoke to your aunt on the telephone early this morning. Your aunt was dreadfully upset. She's offered to help us in any way she can.'

'We had to leave London at a moment's notice.' Fury bubbled in her throat. 'Now we're being dumped on the next train and packed off to Charlbury – '

'Don't make a fuss, Charlotte. You must support me, for your mother's sake. Help me pack this trunk. The hotel will send it on. The staff are being really helpful at this difficult time. Don't let me down.'

They gathered like a band of dishevelled gypsies in the foyer, waiting for a cab to take them to the station: suitcases at their feet, miserable and tear-stained, the twins bickering, Charlotte hugging their shoulders, desperate to protect them from any more bad news.

Her beautiful new frock lay crushed at the bottom of her suitcase.

Tonight, instead of whirling around the floor in Sebastian's arms, she'd be sitting on another train, hot, weary and furious. Lurching through the countryside away from the boy she loved, the twins bickering, Foxie organising more boring sandwiches, everything finished and her beloved father dead.

Why did all the nastiest things in the world happen to *her*?

∽

Sebastian and his family, shining with health, crisp and fresh in their newly ironed linen, marched in an orderly line into the dining room.

Startled and dismayed, Sebastian stared at her.

Behind his mother's back, she raised her hand in a brief, heartbroken farewell.

She managed to mouth one word.

'Goodbye.'

Alexander

By the time Alex had climbed out of the hot tub, towelled himself dry, lurched into his bedroom and slung on some clean clothes, Theo had emptied every bottle of liquor he could find down the kitchen sink. He stood in the doorway as Alex made several futile attempts to comb his hair.

'Don't you worry about all that,' Theo said. 'We're going to the nearest barber shop. I've hired a team of cleaners who will scrub and disinfect every inch of this stinking dump while we're out and remove all those disgusting empties. Then we'll eat a slap-up lunch at my hotel. And then ... '

Theo opened his closet. He ran a disdainful eye over the shabby outfits crammed inside it cheek by jowl.

'We'll buy you some decent new clothes to take on board ship at the Captain's table and then into London and Charlbury. Let's start over from scratch. Socks, pants, vests, handsome pyjamas, tweeds for the countryside, jodhpurs and jackets in which to ride Victor's horses, pale linen outfits for summer afternoons, ultra-smart evening dress. The entire glorious range and anything else that takes your fancy. Think nothing of it, the bill's on me.'

Alex opened his mouth to protest. Too late. Theo had marched him downstairs, waited while he slid on his sneakers and threw on his smelly old coat. He flung a stern arm around him as they hit the street.

The sunlight made Alex blink. The noise of the carriages and clopping horses and shrill voices and harsh laughter roared in his head; the throng of bodies crushed against him. At the barber's, under the hot towel, his beard curling on the floor along with most of his hair, his lungs flapped shut inside him. He almost fainted. He sat upright, wedged his head between his knees, like some pathetic old crone, just to stay alive in the loud, brightly-lit salon full of shaving brushes and lethal silvery scissors. Everyone fussed and flapped around him like startled birds.

They went to lunch at Theo's hotel. Feeling shorn and naked, smelling of the delicious expensive soap exclusive to the best barber in New York, he also discovered he was starving. The scent of rare steak drifted towards him; his heart began to beat properly with each chewed mouthful. Theo grinned approvingly as they made short work of the meal.

Then Theo made him talk about Lillian. What exactly happened? He spelled it out. Sylvia's death … He could hardly say his daughter's name. He had to stop talking before he burst into tears. Was it remotely possible, Theo persisted, that he and Lillian might be reconciled? He shrugged. He didn't know. He'd done his best. He'd loved his wife with every bone in his body. He'd have worked day and night to support her, given her anything she wanted, and more.

But he'd failed. Lillian would always hold Sylvia's death against him. As if he'd *invented* the typhoid virus in a maniac's laboratory to launch it on the world.

Well, fine, Theo said. Make the best of a bad job. Look

forward, not back. Be positive. Other fine fish in the sea. Half an hour of boring advice followed. Alex stopped listening.

Then Theo got practical.

He wanted him to take a six-month sabbatical. He was to contact St Luke's. Ask them to keep his job open until November, without pay. Everything must be above board. Write to his lawyer, tell him where he was going, ask him to tell Lillian. Shut the house, leave the keys with a reliable estate agent, instruct them to look after the property. Collect any valuables, hand them to the bank for safe-keeping. Give his address for the next six months as Theo's consulting rooms in Harley Street, London: a most prestigious location.

If anyone asked, he could maintain a clever front and say he'd be taking a specialised medical course in London under his older brother's watchful and experienced eye. Gynaecology. That should shut them up and no mistake. Who could possibly argue with *that*?

He was forced to agree to Theo's plan. It wasn't as if he had a better one. He spent the rest of the day trailing after his brother, letting him buy clothes in the posh stores along Fifth Avenue, staring at his own skeletal body as he tried on trousers and jackets and shirts and hats, dying for a drink but instead swallowing a gallon of sweet tea and half an enormous chocolate cake, resenting Theo's confidence and panache.

And then suddenly he was completely overcome with fatigue, wanting only to sleep until the cows came lumbering home.

The next five days on the wagon were a total nightmare. Theo never left him alone for a single minute. When he went to sleep, Theo was watching him, covering him up, tucking him in. When he woke, Theo stood there with a cup of steaming coffee and a triumphant smile.

His hands shook, his head throbbed, his heart beat nineteen to the dozen. He felt sick, he couldn't swallow food, he was starving, his blood pressure zoomed off the scale and flopped through the floor. He had hideous nightmares of Lillian clutching Sylvia in her arms while both of them drowned in a neighbour's swimming pool, opening his mouth and shrieking soundlessly for help. He had hallucinations that scared him witless.

Sometimes, first thing in the morning, he hardly dared open his eyes, dreading what his sober mind would imagine. Tarantulas crawling across his bedroom walls. Scorpions emerging from the skirting boards, scuttling towards him to stab his fingers and toes. Cracks in the ceiling widened and danced as he stared at them. His skin itched as he tried to blink the images away. And all the time, sweat poured down his forehead into his eyes.

As he gripped the kitchen table at breakfast, Theo gave him endless boring lectures about liver damage and brain rot and what Pa would have said, and the sooner Al came off the booze the easier it would be. He could have written the lectures himself, word for word.

He knew Theo was right, so he pulled out all the stops and really tried. He could have so easily cheated. Tiptoed out to a Greenwich Village store in the middle of the night and drunk a whole bottle of anything on the sidewalk there and then. But he didn't. Could have bought drugs from a shady dealer in the gutter at the flick of two fingers and the flash of his wallet. But he didn't. Asked a total stranger to buy him cough medicine outside a pharmacy and swallowed the whole caboodle in five minutes. But he didn't.

Instead, he suffered. And boy! It was grimling gibbons.

Theo had no idea how ghastly he felt. Hot and cold. Shivering and shaking. Wanting to laugh and cry at one and the same time.

When he turned to his brother for sympathy, Theo said, 'Tough, dearest bro. You've brought this nightmare on yourself. Now put on your brand new running shoes and go jog around the block. Get the wind in your delightfully short hair and stop thinking about yourself the whole bloody time.

'Here ... I bought you three medical journals, hot off the press. Read them cover to cover. Remind yourself of your true vocation. You're a *doctor*, for heaven's sake. Not a bumbling crawling drunken stupid little sod.'

That brother of his could be real cruel. All he wanted to do was crawl into a quiet hole and die. He didn't have a snowball's chance in hell of doing anything he really wanted with Theo around.

And then, on the sixth day, he woke up and his eyes opened without his having to unstick their glue. He'd kicked the habit. Hallelujah. The thought of liquor made him feel sick. He craved the scent of tea and coffee. He munched his way through a delicious plate of eggs sunny side up and crispy bacon without wanting to puke. Theo could even cook, damn it. Was there *anything* that brother of his couldn't do?

He rolled up the sleeves of his new shirt. Theo grinned at him, pumped his hand until his head rattled. 'Congratulations, dearest bro ... Going back to my hotel.'

The front door slammed, and Alex started making proper plans.

At first he couldn't decide whether he owned anything of particular value for the bank to guard. Then he remembered Lillian's jewellery. Her father was a wealthy businessman who loved nothing more than showering his wife and only daughter with precious stones. Lillian had taken most of her clothes with her. But he'd never checked on anything else.

He sprinted upstairs to open her dressing-table drawer. Its emptiness stared up at him, black and accusatory. She'd taken every fabulous ring, every last brooch, every single necklace. That was the moment he realised she'd left him for good. The fact hit him slap across the face.

And then socked him in the jaw yet again.

He spotted it. The only box that still lay huddled in a dusty corner was one he'd given her on the eve of their wedding. In it sat his special gift from his beloved Grandma: a stunning antique necklace of diamonds encrusted with rubies.

He picked up the box, smeared a finger across its dusty lid, opened it and peered inside. The jewels gleamed at him, catching the light, the diamonds shaped like the curling petals of a flower, the rubies nestled, glimmering berries, among them. He snapped the lid shut.

She could have taken the diamonds with her, even if she'd no intention of wearing them. Leaving them was like her saying, 'You're out of my life, Alex. I want nothing more to do with you.'

He remembered how special his Grandma had always been. They were a family of healers, right from way back when. It was in their blood. Grandma could smell measles just by opening a bedroom door. She'd invented a special potion that cured the most stubborn of warts. She never gave anyone the recipe. People from Kansas and far beyond travelled miles to see her. They'd hold out their lumpy, wart-covered hands. Grandma would tie back her hair and set to work.

'Us women,' she told Alex, 'we're the salt of the earth. We never complain unless there's something really wrong with us. When you've nine children to feed, and you make your living selling tablets of soap and home-made rugs, you ain't got no time to hang about with a sore throat or malinger over a headache. You get up every morning and fight the good fight. See how much you can give to other people before you go to your own bed at midnight, half dead with exhaustion.'

One afternoon a young sailor came to see her. Said his name was Oliver. Nobody else was around. Grandma said he had the nastiest pair of warts she'd ever seen, bar none. Like toads they were, yellow and black and livid green, sprouting on the first finger and thumb of his right hand. She treated him three times.

Within a month he was cured.

He sent her a grateful postcard from Tokyo. For years she kept it pinned to her kitchen wall, until its edges curled and it fell off. Oliver said one day he'd make his fortune, send her a gift she'd never forget. Five years later, the diamonds arrived. Alex watched his Grandma open the parcel, blushing red as a beet when she held the glittering clusters in her hand. Said she'd never have a chance to wear it.

On her deathbed one flaming hot morning, after Grandpa had died and Grandma couldn't find a reason to go on living any more, she'd pressed the jewels into his hands.

'Al, my dearest boy.' Her lips were colourless and barely moved. 'You've always been my favourite. I'm real fond of Theo, but you're something special … Give these here diamonds to your girl on your wedding day. She'll be real lucky to have them.'

So he did.

Fat lot of good it had done him. She'd only worn them that one time, when they said their vows. And now she'd spat them back at him.

Grandma would have been furious. 'Some girls don't know when they've got a good man,' she'd have said. 'You keep them for some other belle.'

He had better plans for them than that.

He'd smuggle them to England, hidden deep in the lining of his new tweed jacket. When he got to London, he'd find an upper-class jeweller and sell them for every cent he could get. Then, while Theo was looking after his ailing women, he'd buy himself real freedom. Take the next ocean liner out on the highest of seas, sail for the land of nowhere, sit on a sunny beach in pants and a sun hat, and drink himself into permanent oblivion.

The diamonds would be his lifeline. Thank you, Grandma.

Then he sat on his bed in the semi-darkness and had second thoughts. What if his jacket got stolen on board ship? He could hardly wear it twenty-four hours a day. Nor could he be for ever checking on its safety, hanging in some unlocked cabin closet.

Even if he *did* manage to get the diamonds to England, what if Theo discovered them and asked why half their value didn't by rights belong to him? What if some snooty English jeweller tried to sell him short? He couldn't possibly haggle. The moment he opened his mouth, his darling Grandma would be there beside him, asking what on God's good earth he was doing. Selling the only family heirloom they'd ever had? Was he *crazy*?

Wait a minute … There was another way.

Len Grant's father was a jeweller. He owned a marvellous shop on Fifth Avenue. He could meet with Len – he wanted

to see him anyway, give him the news, hug him goodbye –
and show him the diamonds. Ask him to give them to
his father. Mr Grant would surely offer him the best
possible price.

His plan worked so well he knew fate had given him its
blessing. He met Len during lunch break near St Luke's the
next day. As he walked into the diner, Len stood up and held
out his arms.

'Great to see you again.' Len's smile told it all. 'You look
a million dollars.'

'Theo bought me some new stuff.' He slumped on to a
chair, his legs shaking like jellied eels. 'Thanks for writing to
him, Len. I've sobered up, big time.'

He told Len of his plans and pulled the heirloom out of
his pocket.

'Holy Moses!' Len sucked in his breath. 'What a
magnificent piece. My Pa will go bananas.' He looked him
in the eyes. 'Sure you want to sell it, Al? Family heirloom
and all that jazz? Promise you won't regret it the minute you
get home?'

'The diamonds will buy me freedom.' He tried to block
out the memory of his Grandma. 'I've promised to go to
England with Theo, but I haven't sworn an oath to stay with
him. Translate those diamonds into hard cash for me, Len.
Then I'll stop fretting.'

Len leaned across the table to grab his hand. 'I'll meet
you here with the money tomorrow. Same time, same place.
Only promise me one thing.'

'Anything. Name it.'

'Keep in touch. Don't disappear off the face of the earth.
Once a month, I want to hear from you. Wherever you end
up, send me a postcard. And if you're in trouble, you're to

let me know. I'll move heaven and earth to help.'

Alex squeezed Len's hand, swallowing hard, blinking back hot tears.

'Thanks, Len … You're a real pal … It's a deal.'

Walking into his bank the following afternoon with all that cash laid out in rows in his new briefcase, he felt like an athlete who'd won an impossible race against all the odds. Len's father hadn't asked any questions – and he'd been more than generous. He handed over enough cash to make the bank clerk sit up extra smart and take notice.

Enough to make his well-planned getaway from Theo when the time was right.

Beatrice

The telephone rang at Chandos Manor that August morning just as Beatrice was about to step into the bath. It was seven o'clock. She wrapped her dressing gown around her and raced down to the hall.

'Beatrice? This is Miriam.'

'How are you?'

'Couldn't be worse. That infernal husband of mine is dead as a dodo.'

'What?'

'He went swimming in Lake Windermere with that trollop. She got into trouble with some nasty old weeds. He rescued her and drowned.'

'Good God, Miriam.' She slumped to the floor. 'I'm so terribly sorry.'

'Yes, well, so am I. I'm also furious and wretched and all over the place. I begged him to give her up, come down to Cornwall, be with his family. Like talking to a brick wall. I've rung Emile at the Porthminster. Did I tell you he decided to be with me a while longer? He'll take me to London on the next train.'

'What about the children?'

'That's where you come in … I was wondering … Would you be the dearest sister ever, and have them and Foxie for me? Just for a few days, until after the funeral, when all the fuss has died down?' Miriam began to cry. 'I wouldn't ask but I trust you. I know the children will be happy at Chandos.'

'Of course I'll have them, Miriam. I need to ask Victor but I'm sure he'll be delighted.' She hauled herself to her feet. 'He'll meet you off the train. Paddington, isn't it?'

'Beatrice, you are an absolute gem.' Miriam blew her nose. 'Emile has just walked through the door. I'll ring you from London … I can't thank you enough.'

The line went dead.

Beatrice skidded into the breakfast room. Three dirty plates and an empty coffee cup stood by Victor's chair. She raced into the conservatory, praying he was still in the stables.

He stood by his favourite new mare, Domino, talking to their groom. Immaculately dressed in his jodhpurs and riding jacket, his eyes widened as he saw her standing by the door.

'Good morning, darling. Have you come for a ride in your pretty little gown?'

She drew him to one side, whispering her news.

'Great Scot!' Victor thrashed his whip against his thighs. 'That sister of yours doesn't do things by halves.'

'No, but none of this is her fault. The thing is, Victor, I've offered to have the children and Foxie for a few days. Here at Chandos. Will that be alright?'

'I don't see why not … Plenty of space, gardens, lovely weather. If it's only for a few days we'll hardly notice they're here.'

'And would you be a perfect darling? Miriam's on the train to Paddington. Could you dash down to London, meet her in the car and take her to Kensington? She's in such a state, and it would make all the difference.'

Victor grimaced, hesitated, and then moved back to his horse. He ran his hand over Domino's gleaming coat, looking into her eyes.

'Got to say goodbye for now, my beauty.' He turned to face her. 'I'd *so* been looking forward to my Saturday gallop.'

'I know, Victor. Thank you *so* much. I'll make it up to you, I promise.'

He grinned, reached out, undid the belt of her gown and glanced at her breasts. 'Fancy a quick roll in the hay?'

She blushed. 'Not with your groom looking on.'

Victor guffawed. 'Too bad.' He bent to kiss her cheek.

'But I promise you better than a quick roll when you get back. Without the hay.'

Beatrice helped him change into his weekend clothes, waved him goodbye and climbed into a lukewarm bath. She'd already decided where her guests would sleep, but all the various preparations needed to be made.

She rang Laura to give her the news.

'Are you wearing black?'

'It's a good question. I haven't had time to think about it. I might have a skirt and blouse here.'

'I'll send you a suit and coat. And Charlotte will need a decent outfit for the funeral. I'll make her one today and send it to Chandos with your stuff.'

'Thank you so much, darling. I'll ring you tomorrow. And I'll be back with you as soon as I can.'

'You were going to have a couple of days' rest, remember?'

'I remember! You know what they say about the best laid plans …'

The travellers walked up from the station that evening, tired and dusty, trailing suitcases. Foxie took the twins upstairs for a bath and supper in their room. Beatrice drew Charlotte into the dining room for a glass of lemonade, a chicken salad and a slice of cheesecake. Over their meal, she gave her niece the details of Harry's death.

'I wanted you to know the truth,' she said, her eyes on Charlotte's pale face. 'There's bound to be gossip. You're not to listen to a word or talk to anyone. The more we contain the prattle, the sooner the scandal will die.'

'My father's been an idiot.' Charlotte pushed her food around her plate. 'He forgot he had a family. He never bothered to write to us at Tregenna. He waltzed off with another woman without a care in the world.'

'He loved you very much. I'm sure the silly affair would have been over by the end of the summer – '

'But we'll never know, will we?' Charlotte gave up on the salad. 'Miriam has this Frenchman in tow. He's got revolting greasy hair and wears perfume. He buys the twins presents, so *they* think he's wonderful. We have to call him Uncle Emile. Uncle indeed! He's a smarmy lizard, always on Miriam's trail.'

Worried by Charlotte's bitterness, Beatrice said, 'Let's have an early night. We'll all feel better in the morning.'

Victor stayed in London for the weekend to help Miriam plan the funeral. The ceremony was arranged for Thursday at St Barnabas Church in Kensington. Leaving the twins in Foxie's capable hands, Beatrice took Charlotte to London on the Tuesday, delivered her safely to Miriam and dashed across London to see Laura.

'It's been a frantic few days. We've tried to keep the twins happy and occupied. Charlotte looks beautiful in the suit you made, but the poor girl is devastated. There's nothing I can do to cheer her up. She adored her father but she can't forgive him.'

'Is Miriam coping?'

'I didn't have time to talk, and her Frenchman was hovering in the hall. At least she has a shoulder to cry on.'

'And what will happen *after* the funeral?'

'I've no idea.' She straightened the cuffs of her black blouse, which she hated. 'I'm praying the press will stay away and give that family space to grieve.'

'The press never behave like decent folk. Miriam's plight is grist to their scandal-fuelled mill.'

Despite its being organised so fast, the funeral went like clockwork. Miriam hid her face behind the heavy veil of a black hat; the ceremony was brief. A few guests gathered in the Kensington house for a buffet lunch, pouring alcohol down their throats as fast as they could within the space of an hour.

Everyone left the house at two. Emile scampered away to meet his publisher. Charlotte vanished with Rosalind. Miriam beckoned Beatrice and Victor into her study.

'I wanted to say thank you.' She took off her veiled hat to reveal a tear-stained face. 'You've both been marvellous. Harry's younger brother, Jonathan, he's still in Calcutta. He cabled saying he's devastated but he can't get away. You two are all I have.'

'Glad we could help,' Victor said. 'It's exactly what families are for.'

'I hope the worst is over, but I fear it isn't. I took Charlotte shopping yesterday. Some wretched journalist spotted us having tea. He's written an article. *Wife and daughter mourn Harry Stallworthy.* I can't even read it.'

'So now they've had their say, there's no more to tell.' Beatrice did not for one second believe it. 'Ignore them, Miriam. While Harry was alive, we never knew what he'd do next. Now – '

'He can't do anything.' Miriam smothered a sob. 'Trouble is, that wretched trollop could decide to sell *her* story. Every time I put my head outside the front door, I come face to face with another vulture.'

'Things will settle down.' Victor patted Miriam's shoulder as if she were a horse. 'Beatrice and I will drive the twins back here to be with you on Monday.'

'Thing is, Victor,' Miriam looked up at him with a crooked smile, 'I've hardly slept, not since Tregenna. Emile says I badly need a holiday. There's a famous spa called Baden-Baden in West Germany. It offers the most wonderful cure for strained nerves. May I go? Would you have the children for a few more weeks?'

Victor removed his hand as if he'd been stung by a wasp. He turned to face Beatrice. 'It's your decision, darling. Could you cope?'

She opened her mouth to say it was entirely *his* call.

'The twins will be off to Eton *very* soon,' Miriam said quickly. 'Charlotte won't be the *slightest* trouble.' Tears bubbled to order. '*Please*, darling Victor. Look after my children for me. It'll be *such* good practice for when you have your own,'

Victor's cheeks flamed orange, then died into livid grey.

'How right you are, my dearest Miriam. Having your brood would be – ?' He glared at Beatrice.

She gave him a wan smile, trying to still her thundering heart.

'We'd be delighted,' Victor said, 'to have them during your much-needed convalescence. Wouldn't we, my dearest little wife?'

The hand, now damp with sweat and anger, descended on *her* shoulder.

'You're going to be *such* a wonderful mother, Beatrice ... I can hardly wait.'

Charlotte

Charlotte felt trapped, caught like a fly flailing helplessly in a spider's web.

She couldn't complain to anyone except Rosalind. Be grateful for small mercies. At least she didn't have to smell the perfumed lizard for a couple of months. Thank her aunt and uncle for rescuing her, a weeping, hard-done-by waif, from the scandalous storm. At Chandos, she must set the twins a good example. Smile, play with them. Not a word about you know who.

Poor little mites. They'd no idea what would hit them. The moment they got to Eton, some ferocious aristocratic know-it-all would point his finger, whisper behind his hand. The questions, the innuendo, the gossip would begin. Family scandals like theirs spread like wildfire, growing more malevolent with every whisper.

Before the twins set off for Windsor, with their new uniforms, tuck boxes and innocent smiles, she agonised: should she take them to one side? Tell them the whole sordid story?

She left their Kensington house fighting hot tears. She liked its high ceilings, its elegant drawing room, the hard-working jollity of Cook and the maids, the sprawling kitchen with its scent of freshly baked bread, the carefully organised busyness of the entire establishment. She loved London, the tree-filled parks, the shops, playing tennis with Rosalind. She had friends here who invited her to parties and were also planning to be presented at Court next spring.

She used to have a whole family.

Not any more.

She was being sent to the country like a parcel her mother couldn't be bothered to open until Christmas. Miriam would enjoy her German watering-hole and Uncle Emile's panting breath so much she'd probably stay in Europe for months.

Would she *ever* see her Kensington house again?

The morning after the funeral, Charlotte and her aunt caught an early train from Paddington to Charlbury. While there were other people in their carriage, they sat in silence. After they got to Reading, they had the compartment to themselves. Auntie Bea took her hand.

As if she'd been rehearsing her words, she said, 'We're going to have *such* a lovely time together. I want to make things more exciting for you at Chandos. Our gardener could build you a tennis court. There's an ideal place at the side of the house, in a field we once cleared to plant an orchard but never did … Would you like that?'

Charlotte nodded, biting her lip. In London she had a best friend with a brilliant tennis coach. At Chandos, she'd have neither and nobody to play with. She gazed out of the train window at the clouds racing against the sky. The fields galloped past, churning up the miles between her and Kensington. London already seemed a world away. She felt like an orphan without a home. It would be so humiliating, being a permanent guest in someone else's house.

As if she'd read her thoughts, Auntie Bea said, 'And if you like, you can come up to London with me on Wednesdays by train, and come back to Charlbury with me and Uncle Victor on Fridays. You could help me with the business. My girls are always delighted to see you. I'll show you my new designs for the winter season. You can choose a party frock for Christmas, and a marvellous evening cape. Would you enjoy that?'

Her patience snapped.

'No.' She sulked like a three-year-old, ashamed of her bad temper but unable to control it. 'If I can't go home to Kensington, what's the point of being in London? I'd rather stay in Charlbury.'

Auntie Bea's shoulders slumped. She'd obviously run out of silly ideas.

Next day, the twins bubbled around in high excitement. Their clothes and books arrived from Kensington, together with their new school uniforms. They scampered along the Chandos corridors, trying on the outfits – Eton suits with large, white, stiff-starched collars – screaming with laughter and joy. They didn't seem to miss Father at all. They'd been told he'd died unexpectedly, that Mother was unwell. She'd gone away to a special place with hot baths to get better.

But they'd got used to not having Father around. They hadn't understood he'd never be coming back. They'd been told Mother would be home for Christmas, but that seemed so far away. In a few days' time they'd be Eton schoolboys. Their wildest dreams were coming true.

While Charlotte was at Father's funeral, Foxie had taken the twins to tea with a family in Oxford whose son was in his third year at Eton. He'd told Blair and Russell a lot about the place.

'The headmaster's name is Edward Lyttelton,' Blair told her over breakfast, waving his fork in the air, trying to look grown-up and important. 'He's a good cricketer and footballer. The college has a funny language. A term is called a "half". The teachers are called "beaks". A class period is a "div". And a "rip"' – Blair grimaced – 'is a piece of work that's so awful it's returned with a rip down the middle!'

'The "dry-bobs",' Russell added, scraps of scrambled egg sticking to his chin, 'are boys who play cricket. Me and Blair will be great at cricket. The "slack bobs" don't do sport of any kind. A "fag" is a young boy who runs errands for the older ones.' He paused for dramatic effect. 'And the most important thing about going to Eton is never to take anything too seriously. Anything at all.'

'Being boring,' Blair said, jumping from his chair and bouncing up and down on the sofa until its springs creaked, 'is the worst sin of all … You're not boring, are you, Lotte? Will you come to visit us at Eton?'

'Of course I will, darling.' She stood up to join him, taking his hands in hers, relishing their soft warmth, loving him for his innocence and energy. She helped him jump off the sofa before it split down the middle. 'Just you try to keep me away.'

The twins were so full of excitement and anticipation she hadn't the heart to tell them about Father. It wasn't *her* job to tell them. She shouldn't interfere. If there was trouble at Eton, the headmaster could handle it. She refused to be their mother, who couldn't even be bothered to see them off to school on their first day.

Uncle Victor, tied up with his bankers' meetings, sent his chauffeur and the Daimler down from London. Auntie Bea, looking wonderful in a new terracotta autumn suit and matching hat – Miriam had forbidden her to wear black – climbed into the car beside the twins. Their freshly packed luggage, piled into the boot, included a tuck box crammed with chocolate cake, shortbread biscuits and creamy fudge.

The twins leaned out of the window. They waved goodbye, their two little faces grinning like the Cheshire Cat in *Alice in Wonderland*.

'Bye bye, Lotte … See you soon … We promise to be good.'

Her heart bled for them.

She turned back to the house, now unnervingly quiet and absurdly tidy. The twins' voices ringing in her ears, she climbed the stairs, wandered into their empty bedroom, and stared out at the silent garden during the loneliest hour of her life.

Foxie kept her going.

She knew her governess missed the twins as much as she did. It was the first time in seven years they'd been separated. Foxie probably longed to be back in London too, but she refused to admit it and stayed resolutely cheerful. She had lessons with Foxie every morning. They both put up a stalwart pretence of enjoying them.

In the afternoons nobody seemed to care what Charlotte did or where she went as long as she was back in time for tea. Every afternoon, even in the wind and rain, she walked in the gardens and across Charlbury's fields.

The village shops lay on their doorstep. She'd race across the churchyard and into Church Street and Market Street, glad to be at the centre of village life. There lived the ironmonger, the shoemaker, the butcher and the saddler, Mrs Allen the elegant draper, the gentleman's hairdresser, the blacksmith, the tailor – and a post office selling brightly coloured boiled sweets and thick liquorice toffees.

Walking past it one afternoon, she decided to write to Sebastian. She'd put *Please forward if necessary* on the envelope, so if he'd left Tregenna someone at the hotel's reception desk would send the letter on. His parents might intercept it, but she didn't care. If she never heard from Sebastian, she'd be no worse off. If he answered, he'd have a chance to tell her something about himself.

And she so longed to know.

She thought about him constantly. If only they'd had the chance to spend time together. She remembered his shoulder brushing hers as they passed on the stairs. The memory of that moment drove her wild.

The following afternoon she walked down the hill and over the bridge to Charlbury station to watch the train pulling in and puffing out. She imagined escaping Chandos, buying a ticket, climbing on board, making her way to Paddington and catching another train to Cornwall.

Waiting for her outside Tregenna would be Sebastian. He'd take her in his arms, tell her how much he'd missed her. They'd walk down to the beach, holding hands; stand by the harbour, watching the boats bobbing, the fishermen hauling their nets, the tide sucking at the sand, the magical silky flowing of the sea.

In her dreams …

That night, she wrote to him. She made several attempts until she got the letter right. She told him why she'd left Tregenna, how she'd adored her father, how she regretted never having a chance to talk to Sebastian properly. She signed it *Your friend, Charlotte Stallworthy.*

She raced into the village the following afternoon, the letter burning a hole in her pocket with two others. Auntie Bea regularly wrote individual letters to the twins at Eton. Charlotte offered to post them. She bought three stamps.

Posting the letters to the twins was easy. She held on to Sebastian's for a long, difficult moment. Then she let it slide.

As the envelope left her hand she prayed it would reach him. Every morning for three days she sat at the breakfast table, longing for a reply.

When on the fourth morning there was one, she felt her cheeks flame hot as a winter's fire. She sat at the breakfast table on her own. Auntie Bea had a headache upstairs; Foxie was busy with chores. She thanked the housekeeper, gulped her tea, left her poached egg lying on its toast and raced up to her room. She sat on her bed, holding the letter. She could hardly bear to open it.

What if Sebastian said she shouldn't have written? What if he thought her pushy? Or he'd forgotten who she was? Worst of all, he might have returned it unopened.

Here goes, then. Time to face the truth.

Tregenna Castle Hotel, St Ives

Dear Charlotte

Thank you so much for writing to me. It was such a surprise. Luckily one of the hall porters handed me your letter without my parents noticing. He gave me a nod and a wink as he did so. That's what I call a good man!

Your letter arrived just in time. We leave for London tomorrow. By the time you get this, we'll be home again.

I'm really glad you wrote. There was a lot of gossip about why you and your family disappeared like that. I hate all that nonsense. I was worried about you. Losing your father must have been terrible. I'm really sorry. Mine's often a pompous old bore, but I love him. Mother dotes on him every minute of the day. I've no idea how she'd manage without him.

Things at Tregenna have been very dull since you left. I'm sick and tired of sea views, walking along the cliffs and getting sand in my shoes. I can't wait to go home. I'm in my third year of reading law at University College London. The new term starts soon and I'm longing to get back to my studies. When I'm old enough and thoroughly experienced, and after I've been called to the Bar, I hope to become a Member of Parliament, like Father.

I'll write to you tomorrow and send you my London address. Stevens, our butler, likes me. He's very good at keeping secrets, so I'm sure I can get him on my side.

Your loving friend
Sebastian Manners

Charlotte clutched the letter to her heart and danced around the room. She flung the window open. The rising sun glimmered in fiery patches through the trees, making the leaves shimmer in red and gold. It was going to be the most glorious day. Sebastian was her loving friend and soon she'd hear from him again.

Over the next three weeks she received four letters from Sebastian, filled with news of his London life, his college friends, the parties he'd been to, his legal studies. She read them with wild delight, hiding them underneath her mattress. She devoured them every night until she knew them off by heart, feeding on them as if they were her only source of nourishment.

Which in a way they were.

She realised she was deeply jealous of him. She tried to fill her own letters with exciting news, but she could summon precious little in comparison to his. He had everything she wanted: a close and loving family, an interesting circle of friends, an exciting course of study. He was ambitious. He knew what he wanted to do with his life. She was merely someone he liked and wrote to when he had a moment. She wondered fretfully where their correspondence was going, if it had any significance – and whether she'd see him again.

Then in the next letter – joy of joys – he suggested they meet. Was she ever in London? Could they get together for an hour over a coffee?

She stood at her bedroom window, hatching a plan. Suppose she accepted Auntie Bea's invitation to go to London with her on Wednesdays? She could watch the pattern of her aunt's day, see whether she might be able to vanish for an hour without anyone noticing.

Auntie Bea was delighted when Charlotte told her she wanted to accompany her to London. And, as it turned out, it was a welcome break from lessons, from the predictable routine of Chandos. Although she couldn't go home to Kensington, being in London was exciting. Laura and the girls welcomed her back. They were putting the finishing touches to a blue velvet party frock Auntie Bea had designed for her. They admired her shining hair and rosy complexion. They told her that Oxfordshire's country air had done her a power of good.

A week later, she went to London for a second Wednesday, carefully monitoring the pattern of Auntie Bea's day. She spent the morning with Laura and the girls, but in the afternoon, after they'd eaten lunch, on the dot of two o'clock her aunt had several private appointments with clients who came for fittings, or with new ones who wanted to discuss their needs.

That was when she could slip away – with luck, unnoticed.

Charlotte sent Sebastian a note, asking him to meet her at the top of Hampstead High Street at a quarter past two the following Wednesday. If it was fine, they could walk on Hampstead Heath and drink tea in a café. She wouldn't have more than half an hour but it would be better than nothing. *So* much better!

Then she threw caution to the wind. She was longing to see him again. Did he by any chance believe in love at first sight?

That Wednesday, she wore her best travelling suit and hat. From the moment she woke, she counted the hours – and then the minutes. As soon as Auntie Bea was with her fashionable lady, and Laura sewing with the girls, she slipped out of the house. The whirr of the sewing machines and the chattering voices masked the click of the front door.

It felt thrilling and even a bit dangerous to be walking alone in Hampstead.

She'd never been on her own in London before. In contrast to walking in Charlbury, nobody gave her a second glance or the time of day. She felt anonymous and free. She could do anything, go anywhere. Not that she wanted to: her feet couldn't carry her fast enough to the High Street.

For a fleeting moment she wondered whether Sebastian would recognise her. The last time he'd seen her she'd looked shocked and tearful in her crumpled summer frock. Now, with a tight-fitting jacket, long skirt, fashionable hat, low-heeled boots, a leather handbag and kid gloves, she felt like a sophisticated young woman of the world.

And of course, she'd know him anywhere. The tall, straight back, that ash-blond head of hair … Any minute now his eyes would catch hers, just like they had that first moment at Tregenna.

She reached the corner of Hampstead station, suddenly overcome with shyness. She stood in the shadows, scanning the faces that emerged from the Underground, hoping the cloudy sky wasn't threatening rain, trying to hold her nerve.

A voice behind her said, 'Miss Stallworthy?'

She spun round, a deep blush flooding her cheeks.

'I hardly recognised you!' Sebastian gripped her elbow, his marvellous blue eyes looking into hers. For the first time, they shook hands. 'You look beautiful.'

She stuttered, 'Am I late? Have you been here ages?'

'Twenty minutes or so. I was early. It's most impolite to keep a lady waiting!'

They laughed. His eyes shone back at her. He continued to hold her hand.

He said, 'Shall we walk? Up to the Heath and back again? Drink the quickest cup of coffee before you vanish to Charlbury?'

They walked slowly, dodging other people, staying in step: past the station, up the steep hill to the Heath. They stared across at London's skyline.

'Do you remember the times we saw each other in St Ives?' She looked sideways at him, their shoulders touching.

'Of course … I wanted so much to ask you down to the beach, or the gardens … Or *anywhere* without our families!'

They laughed.

'Me too.'

'But we've made it anyway. Aren't we clever, Charlotte?'

'I thought –'

'What? What did you think? Tell me.'

'I thought maybe, if you want to see me again –'

'Which I do, very much.'

'My best friend, Rosalind, she lives in Kensington. I could tell my aunt that in future I'd spend Wednesday afternoons with her … It won't be true, but if I arrange things with Ros, tell her about you, it might give us a little more time together, maybe a few hours instead of minutes.' She stared fixedly at the horizon, not daring to look at him. 'What do you think? Can you get away? Do you *want* to get away?'

He touched her shoulder, turned her to face him.

'But of course. I should be studying in the library, my nose stuck in some massive legal tome. I'd much rather be here with you!'

'And your family … If they knew you were here? What would *they* think?'

'Who cares?' He met her eyes. 'I'd risk everything … Wouldn't you?'

'Yes,' she said. 'I would.'

They raced down the hill, not holding hands, but their shoulders bumping together. They drank sweet black coffee in a small café. Then she watched him vanish into Hampstead station.

'Until next week,' Sebastian said. 'Until next week.'

He looked back at her at the station entrance and smiled.

She walked swiftly to Laura's house, grinning at everyone she passed, wishing them a good afternoon, feeling as if she were dancing on air.

Nobody at *A Passion for Fashion* had noticed anything at all.

Alexander

Alexander wrote to Lillian's lawyers, telling them he'd be taking a six-month sabbatical and giving them Theo's Harley Street address. He'd leave the house in Greenwich Village clean and tidy, and in the hands of a regular cleaner and a real-estate agent who'd pay the bills and let him know if any work needed to be done.

He remained acutely aware that the house belonged to Lillian. If she wished to return to it in his absence, she had every right to do so. But he doubted she would. She'd left to escape Sylvia's ghost. He understood. In many ways, he was doing exactly the same. She sent him a telegram:

GOT YOUR NEWS STOP ENJOY YOURSELF STOP
GOING TO ROME SOON STOP THE HOUSE WILL
BE FINE WITHOUT US STOP LOVE LILLIAN

On the eve of his departure he climbed to the attic, remembering how he'd torn up Theo's letter, thrown it out of the window, into the wind. How exhausted and furious he'd been. Now, his anger had burned itself out. He was sleeping like a baby, sober as a judge. Vague plans for his imminent escape swirled around his mind in whorls of increasing excitement. He'd make the best possible use of his freedom.

In the attic, an odd assortment of unwanted furniture littered the floor. He left it as it was. He checked the other rooms. He opened his bedroom closet. It smelled of old liquor and fresh vomit. He gathered the entire contents into a bag, threw it away and scrubbed the closet with the most powerful disinfectant he could find.

The kitchen had already been cleaned almost to extinction. He'd bought crisp white dust sheets which he flung over the furniture in the living room. The spare bedroom was neat and tidy after the few fastidious nights Theo had spent there.

In the nursery, Sylvia's clothes still hung in her closet. Her toys sat in their baskets. Mattie continued to perch on Sylvia's pillow. He didn't have the heart to pack her away. The room smelled of lavender and wax polish. How many hours had he spent sitting on this bit of floor, drinking his bottle of whisky, singing tuneless lullabies, sobbing out his heart to her, night after night?

He said, 'Goodbye, my Sylvia, my darling little girl,' and shut the door.

Alex had looked forward to the first leg of his trip to England on Cunard's ocean liner the *Lusitania*, bound for Plymouth in five days' time, but he hadn't anticipated being seasick for the first miserable thirty-six hours. He lay flat on his back, regularly puking and coughing, his head hot as thunder, their cabin lurching giddily before his eyes whenever he tried to sit up.

Theo ate gigantic meals – describing them in nauseating

detail – played card games on deck, basked in the sun, and danced all evening with the ladies. He attracted them like a magnet. They'd come tapping at their cabin door to ask whether Theo was dressed and ready. Burnished and shining, Theo told them he was ready for anything, flirting outrageously, stringing them along.

'There's safety in numbers,' Theo told him, giving him a ridiculous wink.

When Alex finally slid off his bunk and found his feet, when the cabin had stopped swirling around his eyeballs, he climbed slowly on deck and smelled liquor. Everywhere. At eleven o'clock in the morning, the sherry glasses started tinkling on the drinks' trolley as staff wheeled it between the deckchairs. He had to survive luncheon, drinking only lemonade and coffee, while everyone else sampled the vintage wines whose sweet aromas hovered in the air.

The worst time was six in the evening. Freshly bathed, looking like a stuffed penguin in his new tuxedo and black tie, his dark hair oiled, his fingernails immaculate, he had to sit on his hands to stop himself throttling the nearest waiter and, in a desperate swoop, downing the entire contents of his drinks tray.

In Greenwich Village, Theo had transformed his house into an alcohol-free zone. For ten consecutive days in New York he'd avoided pubs and restaurants, pharmacies selling cough medicine, and grocery stores with their stocks of liquor. But on board the *Lusitania*, there was no escape. The place was a giant floating drinks machine, dripping strong liquor into everyone on board like a leaky tap.

Hell on the high seas, that's what it was.

Reaching dry land at last felt so miraculous he almost sobbed with relief. The sun shone, the clouds raced, the seagulls squawked and squabbled. The crowds on Devon's Plymouth docks looked sane, sober and busy. Theo stood surrounded by women, hugging him, kissing his cheek, pressing their cards into his hand. Alex imagined giving his brother the slip, losing himself and his suitcases in the throng, bobbing in and out among the cabs and horses and trunks and porters and parasols until he'd vanished entirely from Theo's sight.

But first he had to plan his escape in meticulous detail. How clever it would be to play along with Theo's little game until his brother had clean forgotten all about him. Tow the line, he told himself sternly. Hang on in there. Be patient. Theo would soon weary of his little brother, once he was back in Harley Street harness with his ailing ladies, convinced that he'd finally kicked those nasty old habits into the long grass and was behaving like a good little boy.

The train from Plymouth to London was hot and crowded. They laid claim to window seats, their suitcases stuffed under their feet and bulging on the overhead shelves. Theo marched them into the dining car and ordered a three-course meal, followed by strong coffee. Back in their carriage, Theo promptly fell asleep. He'd danced like a hyena until two in the morning, after all.

Alex gazed out of the window as the other carriage occupants left, with their strange clipped English accents. Newcomers climbed aboard. He got a feel for England as the countryside changed around him, imagining where he'd go the moment the time was right.

The Caribbean, and a deserted sandy beach?

A European mountain range that he could climb, fleet-footed?

The art galleries of Florence and Rome? The villas of the south of France?

Meanwhile, Exeter, Bristol, Swindon and Reading flashed by. He read the station sign boards, carefully memorising them. He might need to retrace this exact route in his solo escape.

As the train puffed into Slough, Theo woke, looking crisp and fresh. Their carriage had emptied. For the remainder of the journey, they had it to themselves.

'We'll take a cab to my apartment near Regent's Park and decant our suitcases,' Theo said. 'Then we'll walk to Harley Street and I'll show you my elegant consulting rooms. We'll have supper in town and you can get your London bearings. Tomorrow I'll drive you to Charlbury in my snazzy little sports car. It's back to work for me with a vengeance on Monday morning, so I want to make the most of the weekend.'

'Couldn't we stay in London?' Alex asked plaintively. 'Haven't you had enough of all this travelling?'

'Nope.' Theo checked his reflection in the carriage mirror. 'Five days on the *Lusitania* made a marvellous holiday. Let's round it off in style.'

'The thing about Charlbury,' Theo told him as they drove out of London on Saturday morning, 'is that it's a small English village. *Very* small. It likes to call itself a market town but it's the kind of place where everyone knows everyone. Most of its occupants have never lived anywhere else. Some of them have never been to London.'

'How did you find the place?'

'A doctor friend of mine and his wife used to own my cottage. They invited me down for the weekend a couple of years ago. They'd been offered jobs in Kenya, and wanted to sell it. I fell in love with the place. Offered to buy it on the spot.' Theo glanced at him as he drove. 'My Regent's Park apartment is convenient for my London work, but I only rent it. I wanted to put down a few properly English roots. You'll understand what I mean when we get there.'

'Why have you never married?' Alex asked. The question had been on his mind when Theo had shown him his apartment: it had bachelor pad written all over it. 'Several women on the *Lusitania* were obviously longing for you to get down on one knee.'

Theo laughed, reaching out a hand to pat his thigh.

'I'm well aware of that, dearest bro ... I love women. I get on well with them. I talk their language, I'm fascinated by their bodies, I enjoy solving their problems. I'm always thrilled when one of them tells me how much I've managed to help.'

Theo picked up speed to overtake an ambling horse and cart.

'But at the end of the day, I like coming home to my own patch. Not having to talk about the bodies I've seen, the problems I've solved. I can change gear, switch off and put my feet up with my gin and tonic. My definition of heaven.'

Theo's country retreat was one of the most charming cottages Alex had ever seen.

It nestled in Church Street, slightly larger houses either side of it, as if were content to be a snug fit. The rooms were small but perfectly formed. Comfortable sofas and a small round table with six chairs filled the two living rooms; the bedrooms looked out on to the village street and the walled back garden; the kitchen opened at the back of the cottage on to a neat garden room with a small mahogany desk and two battered leather chairs. The walls were lined with books.

'My small library,' Theo said proudly. 'I inherited the

furniture, but I brought all my books down from London. It's a peaceful haven. I've medical books mostly, all the recent magazines and journals, stuff I'd never have time or energy to tackle at the end of a working day. If I haven't got my head stuck in one of those, I go fishing on the Evenlode, walking in the fields, and of course riding with, or sometimes without, Victor Davenport.' Theo bent to pick up their suitcases. 'I'll introduce you tonight. We're dining with him and his wife at Chandos Manor at seven.'

Alex groaned. 'That means putting on my tux again and sitting on my hands while everyone knocks back the booze … Couldn't you go on your own? I'll take a walk around the village. I'll be perfectly happy here with a bowl of soup.'

'Don't talk twaddle.' Theo made for the stairs. 'I rang Victor last night. He knows you're coming with me and says he'll be delighted to meet you … Come and unpack. Your bedroom overlooks the garden. It's paradise.'

By half past six that evening, Alex had worked himself into a lather of resentment. He was sick to death of his boring tuxedo and formal meals. Theo might have rescued him from a crisis in his life but that didn't make him his keeper. He hadn't even been consulted about dining with Theo's friends. What if they fired questions at him about his job in New York, and why he'd decided to leave?

They might bully him into drinking a glass of wine. He couldn't just sit there and wait for Theo to refuse it for him. He'd have to tell them he never touched the stuff – and then sit back and listen to howls of astonishment. He'd so much prefer to potter around Theo's garden, read *The Lancet*, eat a cheese sandwich and crash out.

He glared at Theo as he walked downstairs, gleaming and immaculate in his evening suit.

'Please let me stay here,' he begged, his fingers ready to undo his black tie. 'I really don't feel like meeting your friends … Tell them I've crashed out with a headache or something. Have a lovely time without me.'

'We'll have a lovely time *together*.' Theo propelled him out of the front door. 'It's a great compliment to be asked to dine with the Davenports. You can't let me down, and I'm not spending the evening explaining your absence. Anyway, you look great in your tux and all. Have I told you how proud I am of you? A couple of weeks ago, you looked like a dog's dinner. Now I'd happily present you to the King.'

Theo pointed towards the end of the road. 'By the way … our local pub, The Bell, serves great English beer and Scottish whisky chasers. But you wouldn't touch either of them with a bargepole, would you?' He dug into one of his pockets. 'Here's your set of keys to the cottage. It'll be your home as much as mine all summer, so make the most of it.'

Reluctantly, Alex followed his brother across Church Street, through the churchyard, past the giant fir tree and the elegant St Mary's church and into the narrow lane behind it. Chandos Manor lay just beyond a line of trees, private and secluded. They were met at the front door by a tall, well-set man with a sleek moustache, dark hair speckled with silver, and an evening suit every bit as smart as Theo's.

He and Theo hugged briefly.

Alex's hand was gripped in a massive clasp. 'You must be the little brother. Alexander, Alex, Al: whichever takes your fancy, eh?' Guffaw at own joke. 'I'm Victor, plain and simple. Victor Davenport. My wife will be down at any minute … Lemme take you chaps out to the stables. Come and meet my marvellous steeds.'

They walked through the hall and a conservatory, out to

a large terrace. Sloping manicured lawns led down to rolling green fields, a river, and glimpses of a railway line threading its way between them. A set of stables sat on their right.

Four horses stood quietly watching from their separate stalls.

'Three geldings and a mare. Diamond and Sapphire were the first to arrive. Jade, this black one here,' he flung an arm out, 'bought him a year later.

'And this is my favourite mare, Domino. Haggled like crazy for her last summer. Ain't she a beauty? Just look at the swirl of colours she carries: black, white and then this marvellous gold. Gets me every time I see her.

'They're all great to ride. I've just sold two Connemara ponies. Bought 'em for my twin nephews. They've gone back to Eton for the summer term. My groom has his hands quite full enough with these four.'

Alex watched while Victor and Theo stroked the animals, cooed into their eyes and examined their legs. He'd always liked and ridden horses. His Pa and Grandpa had been horse-and-buggy doctors in Kansas. They were a useful, friendly way to get from A to B. They weren't pets – and they certainly weren't trophies with names like Diamond. His last Kansas horse had been his much-loved Dobbin.

Ten minutes later, they ambled back to the manor.

And outside the conservatory stood one of the most beautiful women Alex had ever seen. She wore a long blue frock over which the early evening light seemed to flick and flutter in a magical kind of way.

But that wasn't by any means the whole story.

Grabbing his heart-strings were the ivory sheen of her skin, her long neck, the extraordinary grace of her sloping shoulders, the mass of corn-gold hair coiled at her nape, the violet-blue eyes set in a cool, strong, determined face with high cheekbones.   Everything about the woman came together with such perfection it took his breath away. He had to clench his teeth to stop his jaw from dropping to the lawn.

That brother of his! He hadn't thought to mention that Victor's wife was a miraculous beauty. Damn all the saints in heaven, Theo hadn't told him *anything* about her, not a single goddam detail.

For one terrible moment, he was darned if he even knew her name.

Then Victor said, 'Ah, here she is. Darling, this is Doctor Alexander Hertzler, and of course our wonderful Theo back from his travels.' He flung an arm around her, just as if she were a horse.

'Alexander, may I introduce you to Beatrice, my adorable little wife.'

His legs like junket, his heart hammering, Alex held out his hand.

Charlotte

Charlotte discovered that the glittering hour she'd spent with Sebastian – it had flown by on a butterfly's wing – changed her life.

Instead of waking with memories of her father, worrying about how the twins were getting on at Eton, or dreading another dull day at Chandos, her first thoughts were always of him.

She wrote to Rosalind, telling her about the new love in her life. Ros came to tea in Hampstead. She met Beatrice and Laura. Afterwards they walked up to the Heath together.

'All I want is to see Sebastian every Wednesday,' Charlotte explained. 'The Manners are a distinguished aristocratic family. Sebastian's father has an important job in government. But his mother's a frightful snob. She went out of her way to snub us at Tregenna. Sebastian's supposed to be in the library on Wednesday afternoons. If we're careful, nobody will spot us walking on the Heath together or having tea.'

'Of course I'll help.' Rosalind clasped her hand. 'You've had *such* a rotten time and Sebastian sounds like a real gentleman. Tell your aunt you're having tea with me every Wednesday. Send me the dates, so I can cover for you. And sometimes, say on a Thursday, you'll have to *see* me. We'll invent an excuse for a double-day week!'

Charlotte threw her arms around Rosalind. 'I knew you'd come through for me. I'll write to you every week from boring old Chandos.'

Delighted to hear about Rosalind, Auntie Bea gave her cab money to take her to and from Kensington. She also had some money that Miriam had stuffed into her hand minutes before she'd left with Uncle Emile.

Charlotte treated herself to a glamorous haircut at a Hampstead hairdresser, then insisted on paying for afternoon tea with Sebastian. She bought a new hat to wear for their second and subsequent meetings; borrowed a small leather handbag from Auntie Bea. She became skilled at telling her what fun it was to be with Rosalind again.

Her aunt bustled around, busier than ever.

The forthcoming Christmas festivities gave a high dressmaking point to *A Passion for Fashion.* If she wasn't thinking up and sketching new designs and seeing clients in Hampstead, Auntie Bea wrote letters to the twins at Eton, sent them fresh tuck boxes, organised a constant flow of dinner parties for Victor and his banking friends – and designed new outfits for Charlotte.

'I'm delighted to see your new interest in clothes,' her aunt told her happily. 'Miriam will hardly recognise you.'

The actual date for Miriam's return remained a mystery. Every few weeks a letter arrived for Auntie Bea, postmarked Baden-Baden, then Florence, then Rome, then finally Saint-Tropez where Emile owned a villa.

'Miriam sends her love.' Auntie Bea rustled the letters

away and locked her desk. 'She's feeling *so* much better.'

Charlotte had to settle for that. At least the details of the Stallworthy scandal had died down. She prayed the silence would continue.

But it proved to be a blissful break before another storm.

One Friday in November, Uncle Victor arrived in St John's Wood in his Daimler, ready to drive to Chandos. Usually full of smiles at the end of his working week, that evening his face glowered with anger. He ushered them into his study.

'I've just spent one of the most unpleasant afternoons of my entire life.' He lit a Turkish cigarette. 'I want you to know the details before you hear lurid gossip.'

Auntie Bea reached for the nearest chair. 'What's happened?'

'Harry's little trollop has happened, that's what.' Uncle Victor inhaled and coughed. 'She came to see me this afternoon, dressed to the nines, calling herself Lady Armitage. Pretending to be a wealthy client with a pile of dosh to invest.

'She asked for some tea, made sure we were alone in my office. Then told me she was Dora Peberdy. Both the *Daily Mirror* and the *Daily Mail* have offered her money for her story. Asked me to pay for her silence.'

'And did you?' Auntie Bea's face drained of colour.

'Not a brass farthing. I sent her packing even before the tea arrived. I won't be blackmailed by that little tart. If she'd cared for Harry, she'd never have haggled with a daily rag.'

'What do we do now?'

'Nothing. I'll read every paper in town all next week. She may get cold feet, or think better of spilling the beans. She didn't know Harry for long. She can't have *that* much to write about!'

'But it'll stir everything up again, won't it?' Auntie Bea looked close to tears.

'Only if we let it upset us.' Uncle Victor pulled his wife to her feet. 'Come along, my dear. Stiff upper lip and all that. Let's take refuge in our peaceful English countryside.'

'You won't tell Miriam, will you?'

'There's nothing yet to tell.' Uncle Victor squashed his cigarette. 'Of course, Miss Peberdy's arrival and swift departure is already the talk of my bank. I can only hope that's as far as it'll go. That they won't sack me for allowing tarts to pull the scandalous family wool over my banking eyes.'

They spent a miserable weekend.

Uncle Victor didn't want to see any guests. Their Saturday evening dinner party was postponed. He spent Saturday fishing by the Evenlode and Sunday riding all three of his horses. On Monday morning he told Auntie Bea he'd telephone from London if there were any further developments.

There were. The *Daily Mail* had published Dora's story. The telephone rang at Chandos at midday.

'At least it's not defamatory rubbish.' Auntie Bea walked with Charlotte in the garden. 'Your uncle has put a copy of the paper in the post. You don't have to read it, darling. He's still deciding whether or not to tell Miriam.'

'If the article's published there's nothing she can do. She knew this would happen. She deliberately left us to pick up the pieces.'

Auntie Bea squeezed her hand. 'Which we'll do with all the dignity we can muster … The trouble with dealing with women like Dora is that it's tempting to sink to their level in order to beat them at their own game. We must rise above it. Say nothing, do nothing, pray this really *is* the end of the line.'

She couldn't tell her aunt that her chief hope now was that neither Sebastian nor his family ever saw the *Daily Mail.*

She read the article as fast as she could the following day, her aunt standing beside her.

'Quick. Read it and then try to forget it. We'll tear the paper into little pieces. I don't want Foxie to see it. Dora claims that Harry had a string of lovers before he met her, that they'd planned to marry, that he acted like a hero when he saved her from drowning. I very much doubt whether anyone will be particularly interested. Thank God she doesn't mention your mother ... '

But the phone rang that Tuesday evening while they were at supper.

It was the Eton headmaster. The twins had been involved in a series of fights. He asked whether, in the absence of the twins' mother, Mrs Davenport could possibly find time to meet with him and the twins at Eton the following afternoon.

'I've said I'll be with him soon after two o'clock tomorrow.' Auntie Bea's hand shook as she picked up her spoon. 'We'll take the early train to Paddington as usual. I'll put you in a cab to Hampstead, and I'll take one to Windsor.'

'Couldn't I come with you?' Charlotte had to offer, although she desperately wanted to meet with Sebastian.

'No, darling, I'll do this on my own. I never told the twins what had really happened to their father. Maybe that was the wrong decision. I'll talk to them tomorrow, try to find out who they've been fighting with and why.' She met Charlotte's eyes in a blaze of warning. 'And I'm not telling Victor about this. Can I trust you not to tell him?'

'Of course! ... You don't want Miriam to know either?'

'Absolutely right, Charlotte. Thank you for reading my mind.'

She met Sebastian the following afternoon as planned, determined not to tell him anything. But as soon as they were on the Heath, she found herself blurting out the story of the past few days.

He was a sympathetic listener. The details sounded less fraught and lurid the moment the words spilled out of her mouth.

Sebastian promised: everything she told him would remain strictly confidential. They walked back to Hampstead and the teashop holding hands – and when he said goodbye, they almost kissed.

Auntie Bea returned to *A Passion for Fashion* looking pale and shaken.

'I had a long talk with Edward Lyttelton.' She collapsed into a chair and took off her hat. Her lovely corn-gold hair lay flattened with perspiration. 'He's a good man: tall, nice manners, very presentable. He's been extremely patient. Blair and Russell have been in sporadic fights all term, but the one yesterday morning was particularly vicious. He felt it was time I spoke to the twins before anyone gets seriously hurt.'

'What did they tell you?'

'Blair says they've both been taunted. One particular bully keeps telling him his father was a lecher and his mother is a tart. He says it must run in the family and that Blair and Russell will grow up to be crooks and adulterers.'

Charlotte choked with fury. 'Children can be so cruel!'

'Indeed. Russell says at first they didn't even know what the words "lecher", "tart" and "adulterer" meant. He and Blair felt they had to punch the bullies in order to defend the honour of their family! Which made everything worse … Blair has a black eye, Russell a cut lip and a sprained wrist.'

Auntie Bea poured herself another cup of tea.

'I talked to them for an hour. I told them exactly what had happened to their father and gave them a stark warning. If there are any more fights – no matter what names the bullies throw at them – they'll have to leave Eton immediately.'

'You mean, they'll be sent down?'

'Exactly.'

'And dearest Miriam will certainly have to know what's been going on.'

Auntie Bea gave her a faint smile. 'Let's hope it won't come to that. The twins love the school. I think between us, the headmaster and I have managed to bring the boys to their senses.'

Charlotte knew she'd have to survive three weeks over Christmas without seeing Sebastian who planned to holiday in Scotland with his family. She wrote to him every day but was careful not to post the letters until she knew he'd returned to London.

It was lovely seeing the twins again. Both of them had grown several inches, were in high spirits and full of their happier Eton stories. Auntie Bea was careful to warn them not to say a word to their uncle about the fights.

Uncle Victor bought two pale grey Connemara ponies, which the twins instantly christened Sausage and Bacon. He taught them to ride. The sounds of voices and laughter echoed across the Chandos garden and across the fields all through the holidays as the twins rode every morning and afternoon, even in the snow.

On Christmas Day, in spite of the absence of her parents, their small gathering felt like a real family. Laura spent a few days with them. Over the New Year, so did Rosalind. But

Charlotte could hardly wait for the middle of January when she planned to meet Sebastian again. He'd have to work extra hard over the coming months to prepare for his law exams in the early summer.

She'd hoped there'd be news from Miriam of when she'd return. Charlotte's presentation at Court would need several months of preparation. She went to sleep dreaming of curtseying to the King and Queen in a new white frock, her coming-out party in Kensington, and a list of spring and summer dances to which she'd surely be invited. She'd have so much to tell Sebastian!

So the news Auntie Bea delivered one Wednesday morning at the end of February came as a bitter blow. They were on the train, travelling from Charlbury to Paddington in an unusually empty carriage.

'I need to tell you something important, Charlotte.' Auntie Bea chose her words with care. 'Yesterday, I had another letter from Miriam. She can't come home until June or July. Emile is writing a new novel. His French publishers need him to finish and deliver it before he can take time off. Miriam says he's been absolutely wonderful. She can't possibly leave him in France on his own.'

Charlotte's heart began to thunder like a horse finishing a race. 'And what about presenting me at Court?'

'It can't happen this year, darling. It needs months of work, even if I *could* step into Miriam's shoes, which might be officially difficult. I haven't the time to act as your chaperone, organise your party, do everything that's formally required. It's a hugely important social event, and it must be done properly.'

Auntie Bea stared miserably out of the train window.

'There's something else … Your coming out might attract

bad publicity as well as good. I can't guarantee some wretched journalist wouldn't use you to open up those old wounds about Harry's affair and death. As a family, we must make absolutely sure that doesn't happen.'

Hot tears scratched Charlotte's eyes. 'So I'm supposed to hide myself away for the rest of my life because my father behaved like an idiot? It's so *unfair*, Auntie Bea. Rosalind will be presented. We've been planning our parties together.'

'You can still go to hers. I'll take you myself. And I promise to make you the most beautiful new frock for the occasion.'

'It won't be the same. I'll be the poor relation. All my friends will know I've only been asked because they feel sorry for me.'

'But next year, you'll be a star.' Her aunt took her hand. 'Be patient, darling. You've been so brave. You're such a pleasure to be with. I couldn't love you more if you were my own daughter.'

'I wish I *were* yours.' She wrenched out a handkerchief to dry her eyes. 'You and Uncle Victor don't go around behaving like spoilt brats.'

On Wednesday the 5th of April, Charlotte took extra care with her appearance.

Auntie Bea had made her a beautiful spring suit in cream linen with a matching hat. Her tea with Sebastian would be the last time she'd see him for several weeks. He was off with his family again to spend Easter with his grandparents.

Charlotte left *A Passion for Fashion* on the dot of two. Preparations for the Coronation on the 22nd of June were in full swing. All the girls were extra busy. Auntie Bea hadn't even had time to arrange a cab to collect her and, busy with a new client, hardly noticed she'd left.

She walked briskly to the end of Elm Row and turned the corner to Hampstead station, breathless with anticipation.

There was no sign of Sebastian.

In all the months of their meeting, it was the first time he'd ever not been waiting for her. She felt frightened, anxious – and bereft. In her bag nestled an Easter gift she'd bought the week before in Kensington: a sleek tie-pin she hoped Sebastian would love and want to wear with his summer outfits.

So where was he?

What had happened?

She hung about outside the station until half-past two. She'd no idea what to do. Take a cab to Kensington and spend the afternoon with Rosalind? Go home to Auntie Bea's pretending she didn't feel well?

As she hesitated she looked across the road. A woman she half recognised marched towards her, ignoring and only narrowly avoiding a horse and cab. She wore a dress and hat in a hideous deep purple.

'Miss Stallworthy?' Baroness Manners did not hold out her hand. 'Good afternoon … I presume you're waiting for Sebastian.'

Charlotte stared and then remembered. She stuttered, 'Good afternoon, Lady Manners. Yes, of course, I've been –'

'Meeting him almost every week since the autumn?'

'Yes.' Her face flamed with fire. 'How did you know?'

'How indeed!' The Baroness held her ground as a crowd of uniformed schoolboys burst out of the station. 'I found a stash of your letters in Sebastian's room, lying on his bed. I faced him with them. He told me all about your little liaison.'

'We … we met at Tregenna –'

'Please, Miss Stallworthy! I know *exactly* where you first met my son. I haven't come to listen to any details or to spend any more time with you than I absolutely must.'

A pair of furious dark eyes drilled into Charlotte's.

'I've merely come to say you will *not* be seeing Sebastian, ever again. He has serious work to do, and examinations to take. His father and I have mapped out a career for him. There are several young ladies who are already a part of our very select circle who'll eventually make him a most suitable wife. You are *not* one of them.'

A wave of fury crushed Charlotte's lungs. 'Shouldn't the choice be his?'

'It will be, but within strict limits.' The Baroness straightened her hat. It looked even more hideous than before. 'You're to leave Sebastian alone, Miss Stallworthy. There'll be no phone calls, no letters, and certainly no further meetings in Hampstead or anywhere else.'

She gathered up her skirt.

'I hope you've listened carefully to everything I've said.'

'Yes, ma'am. Thank you, ma'am.'

Charlotte could hardly speak.

'I hear you loud and clear.'

Beatrice

She took her sketch-pad into the conservatory, but she sat with it on her lap, staring through the windows at the May-blossomed garden, her mind buzzing with family concerns.

She worried continually about the twins and their progress at Eton, even after a reassuring letter from the headmaster telling her things had settled down.

Miriam's most recent letter had made no mention of her return, but appeared to be dropping hints of another event without describing any specific details. Infuriating as always …

Victor had seemed different lately. He was slower than usual to tell her about his day, less interested than ever before about taking her to bed. Any hope that she might become pregnant floated night and day in her daydreams. But it was beginning to fade into outright resignation: she'd never be a mother.

And today felt particularly poignant. The 6th of May 1911 marked exactly a year since her secret consultation with Theo. She longed to talk to him again privately, but he'd had influenza over Christmas. He'd returned briefly to Charlbury to convalesce, was crazily busy catching up with his patients – and had then suddenly vanished to New York on urgent family business.

She'd done her best to take his advice, but having the twins and Charlotte, much as she loved them, had kept her busier than ever.

She suddenly realised what had changed. She and Victor had lost the language of intimacy. In their early married days, they'd talked so easily together. Gradually it had become an effort. He often asked her when 'that sister of yours' was coming home. He was fond of his nephews and niece – but they weren't his children. The more she leaped to their defence, the more she loved them – and the more resentment she felt towards Miriam.

And now something was wrong with Charlotte. The girl looked pale and miserable over Easter, although she tried to be cheerful with the twins. Their gardener had cleared a patch of lawn beyond the stables to create a tennis court. Charlotte had played with the twins and their new racquets – a generous Easter present from Victor – but obviously missed having her own partner.

Beatrice frowned, trying to remember when she'd noticed the difference. If only she could get the girl to *talk* to her. Every time she tried, Charlotte made an excuse and left Chandos for another long walk alone across the fields. She should have been preparing for her coming-out party. Rosalind had just been presented at Court. It was only natural for Charlotte to feel left out and lonely.

That morning, she hadn't been at breakfast. Foxie said she had a headache, a tummy ache and a slight temperature. Bed rest until she felt better …

Beatrice opened the conservatory doors on to the garden, to hear the magical drone of bees, their gardener's mowing machine on the lawn where it sloped towards the river, the spike of birdsong from the cluster of massive oaks.

She sat back in her chair again. She should be creating new designs for the autumn and winter. Instead she felt a strange paralysis, as if she'd never have another good idea for a new frock, as if she could do nothing for her family but watch and wait and pray. Everything lay waiting – *she* was waiting – for the stillness of that May morning to be broken.

At noon, Victor strode up across the lawn from the stables, flushed with exercise. He took the glass of lemonade she offered and gulped it down. She watched the curve of his throat rippling over the liquid.

'That's better!' He ran his hand over his mouth and took off his hat. 'Jeepers, it's hot out there!'

'How was your ride?'

'Magnificent. Those fields are paradise on earth. Domino's a wonderful mare. Fresh, sprightly, such fun to ride. You should have joined me.'

'You know I hate riding side-saddle … Anyway, I didn't feel like it.'

'Nothing wrong, is there?' Victor's voice tightened.

Beatrice took a deep breath. She thought, Dear God, here we go again.

'Only the usual, I'm afraid.'

'Oh.' The silence of disappointment hung over them. He moved towards her. 'Never you mind, my dear. I know you do your best.'

He brushed her forehead with his lips. She felt the bristling scrape of his moustache. She smelled Domino's scent on his skin and clothes: horse hair, the spray of river water full of young fish, the fragrance of spring grass.

125

New things happening everywhere with the start of spring – except inside her body.

Victor swung away. 'Oh,' he stopped in his tracks. 'I forgot to tell you … Theo rang last night. You'd already gone to bed.'

Her heart leaped. 'That's wonderful news!' She pushed her dreary sketches to one side. None of them passed muster. 'So he's back from New York?'

'He reached London yesterday. He'll be in Charlbury this afternoon.'

'I've missed him. He's been away for weeks. Did you ask him to dinner?'

'Of course.' Victor lit a Turkish cigarette. A lazy haze of smoke drifted on the air. Its sharp aroma cut into her lungs. 'He asked whether he could bring a guest.'

'Oh?' She lifted her chin in surprise. 'Is there a woman in his life?'

'I've no idea. He'll be with his brother, if that's all right with you.'

'Really? Theo never talks about his family. I didn't even know he *had* a brother!'

'His name's Alexander. He's younger than Theo. Much younger … Not yet thirty … Your age, I suppose.'

The smoke hung in the stillness of the air, together with the scent of tar.

She said, 'I'll be delighted to meet him.'

'Excellent, so shall I. He's not a gynaecologist, like Theo, but he's a doctor of some kind or other. It must run in the family. Theo said he'd been in a bad way, this brother of his, but he's much better now. The sea voyage helped. Theo asked us to be specially kind to him.'

Beatrice stood up. She felt dizzy, as if she'd been jolted

from a heavy sleep. 'What an extraordinary thing to say!' She clung to her chair. 'When are we ever anything but kind to our guests?'

'Exactly what I thought. There's something he's not telling us. We'll find out all about it over dinner … I'm off to wash and change.'

'Luncheon in fifteen minutes, then. I'll tell Cook about our dinner guests.'

Victor hesitated at the door of the conservatory. 'Oh, and Beatrice … '

She turned to look at him. 'Yes, dear?'

His eyes were very dark. 'Better luck next time?'

The flush of humiliation rose to Beatrice's cheeks.

'Yes, Victor, of course … Better luck next time.'

A glass of cool champagne to welcome Theo home and greet his brother. Fresh salmon, followed by spring lamb, some good wines, raspberries and cream, coffee and brandy.

An unexpected energy flooded Beatrice as she threw herself into preparations for the evening. She gave a new set of instructions to Cook, made sure the table was set with the best linen, glass and china, cut some lilac for the vase in the hall, tidied the cushions in the drawing room, checked on Charlotte – who was fast asleep – and decided to wash her hair.

She'd wear her violet-blue silk. She'd designed the frock herself; Laura had made it for her. Victor liked it. He said its colour matched her eyes.

Except that as she slid into it that evening, as it rustled against her thighs, as she fastened the deep halter neck, she realised something weird, almost surreal. She was dressing to please a man she'd never met. Her hands shook with anticipation and excitement.

She was as nervous as when she and Victor had given their first dinner party. Since Victor had told her about Alexander, she'd spent the day thinking of, imagining, and wondering about him.

What exactly *had* happened to Dr Hertzler? And what would he be like?

Just after seven o'clock she rustled downstairs.

She heard Victor talking to his guests as he led them through the garden. Showing off his beloved horses before anyone had even been offered a drink!

In the conservatory, the champagne stood waiting in its bucket of ice. Those refreshing bubbles … She longed for a cool glass. Taking Theo's advice, she'd given up coffee and alcohol, but perhaps tonight she'd make an exception and have both …

She drifted out to the garden, taking calming breaths of evening air. She heard the sound of voices again, moving up from the stables.

Suddenly she was surrounded by men: Victor flinging an arm across her shoulders, Theo kissing her hand – and the taller, thinner man standing beside him, bowing his head over their own handshake.

She heard herself saying, 'I'm delighted to meet you, Dr Hertzler … Theo has told me absolutely nothing about you!'

'I'm glad to hear it!' Alexander had Theo's thick, dark hair, swept away from his forehead, the same straight nose and firm mouth. But his eyes were an extraordinary light grey that seemed to darken as she looked into them.

'Welcome to Chandos Manor.'

'Thank you for inviting me, Mrs Davenport.' His voice had that same wonderful American drawl she loved in Theo's voice.

'Please, call me Beatrice.' His hand was still in hers, then it slid reluctantly away. 'We never stand on ceremony.'

Victor cut in, 'Indeed we don't … Is that iced champagne I see?' He picked up the bottle. 'Let's make short work of it.'

But when he was offered a sparkling glass, Dr Hertzler clenched his hands behind his back, politely but firmly refusing. Relieved to have an excuse not to waste it, Beatrice drank it instead. The bubbles fizzed into her throat and then her mind.

She spent the meal looking after her guests, making sure their plates were full, their glasses replenished. The various courses followed like clockwork, each perfectly prepared. Conversation flowed across the table. A notorious Charlbury poacher had finally been captured and hauled before an Oxford court. Victor faced several new banking problems in the City. Theo described what it was like being back in New York after five years' absence.

But she hardly took part.

She watched Alexander Hertzler carefully. He ate only half the delicacies on his plate, refused the wines and drank glass after glass of lemonade. Briefly, he answered the mundane questions he was asked, but it obviously came as a relief when nobody spoke to him and he could sit in silence.

She wondered whether he really wanted to be with them; whether he'd only come at Theo's insistence or because he'd nowhere else to go. She desperately wanted him to enjoy being at Chandos – and at her side.

Victor and Theo ate and drank a great deal. At the end of the meal, reeling gently and replenishing their brandies, they disappeared to play billiards in the games room like two little boys at a party.

On the spur of the moment, she offered to show Dr Hertzler the moonlit garden. She wanted to be alone with him: to listen to a new voice telling her about new places.

He agreed with alacrity.

They walked in uncomfortable silence down to the cluster of oak trees that led on to the fields and the river beyond.

'How dark the sky is behind those stars, away from city lights!' His soft voice seemed to caress the air. 'Velvety black! And how quiet it is. If I threw a pin on to the grass, I'm sure I'd hear it fall.'

Gratefully, she seized on the neutral territory. 'I remember the day I first saw Chandos Manor, just over four years ago. Victor drove me down from London in his Daimler. I'd never been to Charlbury before. I thought it was the most peaceful place on earth.'

'There's a difference between a silence that presses on your ears, and peace, isn't there? I spend my life in St Luke's Hospital that never stops working and the city of New York that never sleeps.

'I've just stepped off an ocean liner. You'd think *that* would be peaceful enough if you found a solitary corner on an empty deck. But there's always the roar of the sea, the rumble of the ship's engine, somebody's raucous laugh from behind a cabin door.

'The only time New York is really quiet,' he hesitated, 'is when there's been a snow storm. The heavy white blanket is ghastly. It muffles the place, suffocates it for a week, maybe two. Then everything thaws and bedlam returns. But while the blanket *is* there,' his voice trembled, 'you can scream your head off and nobody will hear you.'

'I'm still a Londoner.' Beatrice turned to face Chandos, admiring how its lit windows shone into the darkness. 'I'll never be a proper country woman. I love the pace and excitement of the city. I only spend a few days every week here, at weekends and the start of the week.'

'Aren't you ever lonely?'

The question took her unawares. He was watching her, waiting for her response. How on earth had he spotted the truth so swiftly?

She said defensively, 'Why do you ask?'

'Forgive me.' He dropped his gaze. 'I'm getting personal and we've only just met ... You and your husband seem an odd couple. You're so much younger, so much less' – he searched for the word – 'conservative.'

She laughed. 'You're much too perceptive, Dr Hertzler.'

'Then I'm right!' Laughter rang in his voice too.

'I suppose you are in a way.'

'How did you meet?'

She thought back to that entirely unexpected day. 'Through my business partner, Laura Brightman. We run a fashion business together. One of her cousins got married in London. It was a huge affair, money no object. We designed and made the bride's wedding dress and frocks for the two bridesmaids: three-year-olds with roses in their hair. They looked adorable.'

She paused, remembering.

'Go on.'

'We'd arrived at the wedding reception. I was kneeling besides the bridesmaids, smoothing their skirts, making sure their roses were firmly pinned. I noticed someone looking at me. It was Victor Davenport, standing in a corner, staring at me. I recognised him from photos in society magazines.

'He introduced himself, insisted I stay to luncheon. We talked all afternoon. Then he took me home. In the car – his chauffeur drove us, it was all very formal – he said he wanted to marry me and have lots of children.'

'Phew!' Alex caught his breath. 'Quick work! A man who knows his own mind.'

'Indeed. That sums up Victor perfectly. He's very sure of himself.' She turned her head away. 'And of me.'

'And so you married him.'

'Three months later, I made my *own* wedding dress! He swept me off my feet. I hadn't been looking for love, but I was twenty-five and I wanted children. Offers from men of Victor's calibre don't often arrive in a woman's life. He was very persuasive. I was flattered – and ready to take the risk. The only condition I made was that I could keep working at *A Passion for Fashion*. Laura and I had been students together at The Slade School of Fine Art. We made a pact that marriage wouldn't split us up. And so far, it never has.'

'So who's more important to you, Mrs Davenport? Your business partner or your husband?'

The audacity of the question made her catch her breath.

'I can't answer that … nor should you have asked!'

'I'm sorry, I've gone too far – '

'Yes, indeed.' Stung into hostility, she wanted to get her own back. 'Are *you* married, Dr Hertzler? Could *you* choose between your wife and your job?'

There was a long silence. As if the sounds came from a long way off, Beatrice heard plates clattering in the Chandos kitchen, the steady plash of the river, the shriek of an owl swooping over the stables.

Alex said, 'I don't have the luxury of choice. Six months ago, my daughter died of typhoid fever. My wife also caught the disease. We were trapped in the snow in New York … It was the most terrible night of my life. My wife never recovered from – '

'Good *God*, Dr Hertzler, I'm so sorry. I had no idea … Theo told me nothing about you. I'd never have asked you such a question if I'd – '

But instead of finishing the sentence, she heard a voice calling from the house.

'Mrs Davenport!'

Foxie stood in the conservatory doorway, silhouetted against the light. She waved an arm and began to stumble across the lawn.

'Foxie … Whatever's the matter?'

'Please, could you come quickly … It's Charlotte. She's doubled up in pain, clutching her stomach, asking for you.'

As if it were something she'd done a thousand times, Beatrice turned to the man standing beside her.

'Could you come with me? Charlotte is my niece, but I love her as if she were my daughter.'

'But of course.' Briefly, Alex touched her bare shoulder. His fingers seemed to throw a bolt of electricity through her body. 'Show me the way.'

They raced into Chandos, through the conservatory and the hall, upstairs and along the corridor. Charlotte's door stood open. She lay on her bed, moaning with pain.

Beatrice bent over her and took her hand.

'Charlotte, darling … This is a friend of ours, Dr Hertzler. He's Theo's brother. He's offered to help.'

Alex perched beside her. 'Hi, Charlotte … My name's Alex … May I take a look at you, please? … Could you lie flat on your back for a moment?' He felt her pulse, placed the back of his hand on her forehead. 'You have a very high fever … Show me where it hurts.'

Charlotte stared up at him. 'Mostly here,' she grimaced. 'And here.'

'In the centre of your abdomen? … And the lower right side? … How long have you had the pain?'

'Since yesterday. I've had no appetite. I couldn't eat anything.' Tears glittered in Charlotte's eyes. 'This morning it was bad. I felt sick. When I tried to walk my tummy hurt. I fell asleep this afternoon, but when I woke up it was much worse. My insides are going to explode.'

Alex stood up. He looked directly at Beatrice, a straight, stern glance that made her quail. 'Charlotte has appendicitis. She has a high fever, and the area of pain would indicate it for certain.'

Beatrice gasped. 'What should we do? If we leave it until morning – '

'It's much too dangerous to leave, even for an hour. Let me drive Charlotte to hospital. Do you have a car?'

'Victor has a Daimler. Can you handle it?'

'I can drive anything from a farmer's truck to a Cadillac. Where's your nearest hospital?'

'There's one at Burford, but it's small and may not have the right staff for a night-time operation … Oxford's our best bet, the Radcliffe Infirmary.'

'Do you know the way? Can you guide me?'

'Yes. I do and I can.' Something occurred to her. 'Have you driven in England before? Remember: we use the left-hand side of the road!'

'I know. It felt very odd when Theo drove me down. I promise to remember.'

She broke the spell between them. She turned to Foxie.

'Could you let Mr Davenport know what's happened? He's playing billiards with Theo. Ask him to telephone the

Radcliffe immediately … He's to tell them we're on our way and they're to be ready for us.'

Alex seized Foxie's hands. 'You couldn't possibly have known how serious this is. Tell my brother I'll find my own way back to his cottage later tonight. He's not to wait up. He's given me a key.'

He bent towards Charlotte. 'You have nothing to be frightened of. You're in safe hands and you're going to be just fine.'

In a gesture both simple and beautiful, he scooped Charlotte into his arms.

Charlotte flung hers around his neck. Her pale face, distorted with pain, lay on his shoulder. Her dark hair tumbled down her back. The sleeves of her dressing gown slithered to her elbows, revealing a flash of skin. Her small bare feet made her look like a waif being rescued from a storm.

To Beatrice's horror, a stab of jealousy knifed through her heart. For an instant, more than anything in the world, she too wanted to be lying in Dr Hertzler's arms.

Beatrice

She reached across the crisp linen sheet and took Charlotte's hand in hers, the surgeon's words echoing in her head.

'You can see her now, Mrs Davenport, but not for very long. She's still under sedation, so she'll be drowsy. Though glad to see you, I'm sure.'

The small hospital room lay in semi-darkness, but she could see Charlotte's pale face and long dark hair clearly enough, and hear the soft, measured intake of her breath. At the pressure of her aunt's fingers, Charlotte opened her eyes.

'How are you, darling?'

'Auntie Bea … I'm a bit sore, but the terrible pain has gone.'

'The operation was a great success. I'm so proud of you. You've been very brave.'

'I didn't have much choice, did I?' A brief smile flickered across Charlotte's face. 'Everything happened so fast – '

'It had to, or you'd have been in real danger.'

'Thank you for taking such good care of me.' Charlotte licked dry lips. 'It'll be a great story to tell the twins. They can dine out on it for weeks.'

'They will indeed!' At least it would be a scandal-free story to tell. 'They'll want to know all the details.'

Charlotte shifted uncomfortably under the crisp sheet. 'Is Dr Hertzler – '

'Yes, of course. He's right here – '

'I sure am.' His voice came from a shadowy corner.

Beatrice gestured to him to come closer. He stood opposite her, taking Charlotte's hand in his. She looked across at him. They both still wore evening dress. She had hastily grabbed a wrap to cover her long frock. Dr Hertzler had taken off his black tie so that his white shirt flared open at the neck. They looked oddly extravagant and over-dressed in the hospital's Spartan surroundings.

'Congratulations, Charlotte. I've spoken to your surgeon. The operation was casebook perfect. You're going to be just fine.'

'If it hadn't been for you – '

'Nonsense. Only doing my job. You must rest. Eat and drink plenty to keep up your strength.'

Charlotte's eyelids drooped. 'All I want is sleep.'

'Of course.' Beatrice kissed her cheek, reluctant to leave but suddenly exhausted. 'Uncle Victor and I will come to see you later. He'll be so delighted to hear the news. Sleep well.'

'Auntie Bea …'

She turned at the doorway. 'Yes, darling?'

'I don't want Mother to come. You won't tell her what's happened, will you?'

'I'll have to write to her. I can't just pretend – '

'But not yet. Not until I'm back at Chandos. And don't send any telegrams. Please, Auntie Bea. I don't want her rushing to my bedside.' Charlotte clutched the sheet. 'And I couldn't *bear* it if she brought Uncle Emile with her.'

Beatrice sat beside Alexander in the Daimler as he drove slowly back to Charlbury, a pale Sunday-morning dawn creeping into the sky.

Tired, their nervous energy spent, they remained in companionable silence until they reached the outskirts of Charlbury. Once she was home, this totally unexpected, frightening but somehow magical interlude between herself and the man beside her would be over. She dreaded their parting.

She broke the silence. 'I don't know how long the hospital will want Charlotte to stay, but could you come to see her with me later this week? I'm sure she'd want to see you.'

He turned to look at her. 'I'd be delighted.' He hesitated. 'How will you make the journey in the meantime?'

'I'll ask Victor to travel to London by train, leaving me his chauffeur and this Daimler. He's not going to like it, but my need is greater than his.'

'Don't you drive?'

'No. I've always promised myself one day I'd learn.' She bit her lip. 'When we were first married, I used to have a recurrent nightmare. Chandos was full of children, one of whom was taken ill and needed my help. I'd rush out to a waiting car, then realise I didn't have the first idea how to handle it. I'd wake up terrified, furious at my inability to cope with an emergency.'

Alex said slowly, 'I've just had a marvellous idea.' He was looking at the road ahead, but she saw his smile. 'If it succeeds, it could solve a lot of problems. But I'm not going to tell you what it is until I've put it into action.'

He swung the car into the Chandos driveway, stopping in front of the house. He turned to look at her, his eyes dark, his hair tousled, his open shirt revealing a neck she suddenly longed to touch.

'For the moment, then, good night, Beatrice. Or should I say good morning after our long and rather wonderful night together?'

'What can I say?' She blushed beneath his gaze. It was the first time he'd called her by her first name. 'You've been the hero of the hour.'

'Only too glad to be of service.' He ran a hand through his hair. 'I'm going to London tonight with Theo to put my plan into action. But the moment I'm back in Charlbury, I'll call to see you. It'll be Wednesday, Thursday at the latest.'

'I'll be waiting.'

They climbed out of the car. She watched as he strode away.

The full circle of a fading moon beckoned to her. Dark forebodings clutched at her heart. What if something happened to him in London to prevent his return? What if he got caught up with other activities, met new, scintillating people? What if he decided to stay? What if they were destined never to meet again?

Shivering at the thought, and at the damp dawn air rising from the wakening garden, she let herself into the house. It slept in secret shadows. No twins – she'd got used to them being at Eton – but now no Charlotte either. She'd have to face the week alone, with only Foxie for company.

She began to climb the stairs as the study door rattled open. She turned to see Victor in his dressing gown, holding a glass of brandy. She could smell the liquor from where she stood.

'And what time do you call this?' His voice came cold and quiet.

She clutched the banister, her exhaustion hardening into anger. 'We had to wait until Charlotte's operation was over and I could see her.'

'And how *is* your dear niece?'

'Absolutely fine.' She ignored the heavy sarcasm. 'The operation was a complete success. I saw her briefly and I've left her to sleep. I told her we'll be back to see her this afternoon. She's been really brave, Victor. She was in a lot of pain.'

'It's been a painful episode for *all* of us, Beatrice. Come into the study for a moment. I need to talk to you.'

'Can't it wait until breakfast? I'd really like to snatch a few hours' sleep.'

'No, it can't wait. Let me tempt you with a brandy.'

She followed him into his study and closed the door.

Victor stood with his back to her, pouring a drink.

He said quietly, 'This has got to stop.'

'I beg your pardon?'

He swung round to face her. 'I said *this has got to stop!*'

The alcohol swirled in the glass. She moved towards him, took the drink and raised it to her lips. The brandy stung her mouth, put fire in her belly.

'What are you talking about?'

'Your chasing around the countryside in such an undignified fashion at all hours of the day and night, rescuing your sister's children from their various emergencies. It must *stop right now.*'

'Don't be ridiculous, Victor!' Fury gripped her. 'What would you have me do? Leave Charlotte to die of peritonitis in one of our bedrooms?'

Victor flung out a hand to silence her. 'First the twins behave so badly at Eton you have to endure a humiliating interview with the headmaster, like some silly little schoolgirl who's been caught smoking in a midnight dormitory. Oh, yes, I knew about the incident … I keep more of my ear to

140

the ground than you realise, and I'm well aware you chose to tell me nothing about it.

'Now Charlotte's ill. You throw yourself into my Daimler and vanish, leaving me to face a hysterical governess who can hardly get a sensible word out of her mouth. You then spend the entire night with a man you've only known for half an hour.'

'Don't be absurd, Victor! Dr Hertzler is Theo's *brother* – '

'I don't care whether he's the Prince of Wales! You gave me no warning whatsoever. You didn't even bother to ask my permission.'

'There wasn't *time* for anything. We had to get Charlotte to hospital – '

'I could have driven you. Why didn't you ask *me*?'

'You'd drunk far too much at dinner to be able to drive anywhere.' Her voice shook. 'Dr Hertzler was stone cold sober. He made his diagnosis and wanted to follow it through as swiftly as possible. We're talking emergencies here, not invitations to a Royal garden party ... Anyway, you were playing billiards with Theo. I had no wish to disrupt your evening.'

Victor turned away from her, flinging himself into a chair. 'All that aside, I'm not prepared to tolerate this situation a minute longer. You're to send Miriam a telegram telling her to come home immediately to look after her own children, face up to her responsibilities and behave like a proper mother.' He gulped his brandy. 'If you don't, I will.'

Her legs started to shake. She put down her drink, held on to the back of a chair. 'Charlotte specifically asked me not to tell Miriam.'

'And why would *that* be, I wonder? I don't suppose it has anything to do with the perfumed Frenchman your sister trails around with? I gather Charlotte dislikes him.'

141

'It might do.'

'I see.' Victor's voice was icy now, his eyes dark with fury. 'And you consider Charlotte's wishes to be more important than mine?'

'Of course not, Victor. But the aftermath of appendicitis has to be treated with great care or there can be complications. I want Charlotte to be perfectly well and back home with us before I write to Miriam.'

'By which time the worst will be over, and your sister can safely assume there's nothing more she can do!'

This was so exactly what Beatrice wanted that she remained silent, surprised by how much she looked forward to nursing Charlotte back to health. The fact that it also gave Alexander Hertzler a cast-iron excuse to visit Chandos with impunity swam vividly into her thoughts.

Victor stood up abruptly. 'I'll go to see Charlotte with you this afternoon. I hope your niece recovers swiftly. I'm happy to pay for her medical and nursing care, and I'm glad she'll be able to return to Chandos. You may have the Daimler and my chauffeur for the whole of next week.'

Trying to pour diplomatic oil on troubled waters, she murmured, 'Thank you for your generosity, Victor – '

'But none of that alters my resolve. I *insist* that Miriam resumes her maternal duties, whether she wants to or not. I shall send your sister a telegram the moment I get to the bank on Monday morning.'

He walked brusquely past her, out of the room. But he paused at the open doorway to look back at her.

'By the way. That governess Miriam employs. She's hardly pulling her weight, now, is she? The twins are at Eton. All Foxie ever seems to do is read endless novels with Charlotte for a couple of hours five mornings a week. We've been housing and feeding her for months. I really think the

142

time has come for her to leave. There must be a hundred other jobs she could go to. I'm perfectly willing to write her a decent reference ... Good night to you, dearest wife ... Or should I say good morning?'

Beatrice sank down on a leather armchair in the empty study. She drank the brandy in short gulps, her hand trembling with exhaustion and her heart with panic.

Victor would feel better after forty winks and a hearty breakfast. She'd no intention of meddling in Foxie's future. She'd do everything in her power to persuade him to leave Miriam alone. The moment he saw a pale but smiling Charlotte in her neat hospital bed his heart would melt. It could only help her cause.

But it didn't. Courteous and polite to Charlotte, he was aloof with her in the Daimler on their journeys to and from the hospital – and stubbornly adamant when she raised the subject on Sunday evening.

At breakfast on Monday morning, she tried one last time.

'If you love me, Victor, you'll say nothing to Miriam.'

Her words hung over the table like the ominous rumblings of a thunderstorm.

Victor raised his head from his newspaper and looked her in the eyes.

'It's precisely *because* I love you that I shall not change my mind.'

She watched from the window as he strode off to the station.

He hadn't kissed her goodbye. He hadn't said he'd telephone. He obviously didn't hope she'd have a pleasant week. Any further pleas would fall on deaf ears.

Gritting her teeth, she ploughed on with her morning's

chores. She needed to clear the week ahead so she could be free to see Charlotte every afternoon. She rang Laura, told her what had happened, and asked whether she could postpone her appointments on Thursday and Friday.

She noticed a miserable-looking Foxie loitering in the hall, and asked her whether she'd like to visit Charlotte with her that afternoon. Foxie's face lit up with a smile. She consulted Cook about the week's menus. She asked the maids to spring-clean Charlotte's room, make up her bed with fresh linen. She walked in the garden, picked daffodils to take to Charlotte's bedside.

And all the time she imagined Victor sending Miriam his telegram – and wondered what Alexander was doing in London.

The following morning, Chandos felt unnervingly quiet. She'd heard nothing from Victor. She still hoped he'd thought better of his telegram. She wandered out to the conservatory and then the gardens, trying to find the energy to work on some new designs.

At eleven o'clock she walked back to the house, desperate for some shade and a cup of coffee. Foxie stood in the conservatory doorway, holding a telegram.

'This has just arrived for you … I hope it's not bad news.'

Beatrice took it from her with shaking hands, sat down on the nearest chair and opened it.

DEVASTATED TO GET VICTOR'S NEWS
OF CHARLOTTE STOP CANNOT COME HOME
IMMEDIATELY STOP EMILE AND I ARE MARRIED
STOP EXPECTING FOURTH CHILD NEXT MONTH
STOP DOCTORS FORBID ME TO TRAVEL STOP
LETTER FOLLOWS STOP LOVE MIRIAM

Alexander

Alexander walked slowly through Charlbury in the dawn of that Sunday morning, feeling the crisp air against his face, remembering the events of the night almost as a series of snapshot photographs.

Driving carefully along the country lanes, following Beatrice's instructions, up to the hospital gates.

Lifting Charlotte out of the Daimler and carrying her through the doors.

Seeing Beatrice's worried face as she spoke to the doctors.

Waiting with her for the duration of the operation, talking to her about anything and everything, longing to take her in his arms to comfort her.

Watching her bend over Charlotte's pale face, relief and love shining in her eyes.

The sound of her voice echoed in his head. He imagined touching the long, clean sweep of her arms, undoing the coil of her hair, running his fingers through it. Kissing her lips.

He imagined many other things but hardly dared admit them.

He let himself into Theo's cottage, tiptoed up to his room. He dropped his clothes to the floor, just taking in the chirp of early birdsong from the trees. He flung back the eiderdown and dropped like a log into the cool linen sheets.

Within seconds he'd fallen asleep.

Theo woke him at midday with a cup of tea. Alex grinned up at him from his pillow.

'Well, now, dearest bro,' Theo said. 'You've scored a palpable hit. I've just spent a couple of hours riding with Victor. I spoke to Beatrice as I left Chandos. I thanked her for giving us such a lovely evening. She tells me you were quite the hero of the hour.'

'I did my best. And Charlotte stepped nicely up to the mark.' He gulped his tea. 'We seem to be rather good at rescuing damsels in distress.'

'You didn't waste much time!' At the door, Theo turned to face him. 'And this from a man who had to be dragged kicking and screaming to that dinner party by the scruff of his reluctant neck. What are you planning for your next trick?'

'I'm coming with you to London. There are things I have to do.'

'Oh? Sounds mysterious. Spill the beans.'

'Not until I've put them into action ... Do you by any chance have a useful map of the great city?'

Theo frowned. 'Not here in Charlbury. But I can find you something when we get to Regent's Park.'

Alex swung his legs over the edge of the bed. 'There's something I *do* have to tell you. While Mrs Davenport and I were talking in the garden, I may have given the impression that I do not have a wife.'

Theo stared. 'You mean – '

'I told her my daughter had died of typhoid … I had every intention of telling her about Lillian, but we were interrupted by their governess. We had to rush to Charlotte's bedside. Beatrice probably assumed that my wife was also dead.'

'So you lied to her – '

'Not exactly. Anyway,' Alex's voice gathered bitterness, 'Lillian's still in Rome, isn't she? She doesn't care enough about me to come running into my arms. She's more concerned about her father's health than mine.'

'My dearest bro.' Theo frowned. 'You're splitting the finest of hairs.'

'Yes.' Alex stretched his arms above his head. 'And now there's no going back. You must promise not to give me away. Mrs Davenport doesn't need to know one way or the other, does she now? It makes absolutely no difference either way.'

As Theo drove them to London that evening, Alex wrote down the route he took. It still felt strange to be driving on the left. He asked Theo where he'd bought his car, listening carefully to the details of the showrooms in St John's Wood.

Next morning Theo faced him squarely over the breakfast table, already immaculately dressed. 'I can trust you, can't I?'

'To do what exactly?' Still in his cotton pyjamas and robe, he felt the familiar hackles rise at the patronising concern in Theo's voice.

'To stay off the booze.' Theo folded his newspaper and crisp serviette. 'I'm due in Harley Street and then the hospital. I shan't be home until after six. London has a thousand pubs, some shabby, some glamorous. All packed to the rafters with liquor. You're to promise me none of it will find its way down your throat ... Please, Al. You look so much better now you've – '

'Come off the wagon.' He flushed. 'I'm over the worst, and it was pretty grim getting here. There's no way I'd put myself through all that, ever again.'

Theo's face shone with relief. 'Pa would be so proud of you. Have a great day, Al. Explore the sights. Museums, art galleries, shops ... Tell me all about your adventures tonight.'

Alex left Theo's apartment at ten o'clock, intent of purpose. The art galleries could wait. He had more important business to transact.

He wore one of the dapper town suits in pale grey herringbone tweed that Theo had bought for him in New York, with a crisp tie, polished shoes and a black hat. The more he looked like an English gentleman, the more successful would be his day.

He walked slowly through to Oxford Street and hailed a cab. It took him to the bank on The Strand where he'd already arranged to set up an account. Unprepared for the marble-pillared elegance of the place, its black-and-white-tiled floors and air of long-standing prosperity, momentarily daunted, he had to spur himself on.

His money was as good as any of the swanks around here, wasn't it?

Wearing his new outfit certainly helped. He doffed his hat with confidence. Having the name Hertzler certainly helped too – Theo was obviously a well-known customer – as did being able to give a distinguished Harley Street address and pretend he was on a medical working sabbatical.

And the money from those diamonds sat as a substantial, as yet untouched, amount that no aspiring bank clerk could query. He left the bank with both cash and a new cheque book in his pocket, feeling like a prince among men.

On the steps outside he hesitated. Should he find a coffee and something to eat before he went to the car showroom in St John's Wood? He decided the midday refreshments could wait, and turned to hail a second cab.

Which is when he heard a familiar voice and hearty laugh. He glanced over his shoulder. Victor Davenport was guiding an exquisitely dressed woman across the road, his arm flung protectively across her shoulder.

He'd clean forgotten the man was one of the bank's directors. He fought his feelings of revulsion. The woman was probably one of Davenport's clients. They must have had a business meeting and were going out to lunch. The situation must surely be above board. Davenport would hardly two-time his wife in such a public place. Would he?

He shrugged his shoulders. He wasn't going to waste the precious hours of his first day of freedom in London by worrying about how Beatrice's husband spent his time. Smothering a surge of bitter jealousy, he hailed the nearest cab.

He pressed his nose against the showroom window. He saw it immediately. His eyes went straight to the car as if the motor had been waiting for him and him alone. His heart missed several beats.

It was a small but perfectly formed Rolls-Royce, with pale cream paintwork and the famous mascot: the elegant winged figure leaning out to face the sun, the wind and the rain. He could hardly wait to see it at close quarters.

He pushed at the showroom's door.

Inside the hushed surroundings he moved towards the car as if it had magnetic properties. Its maroon leather seats looked snug and cosy; the dashboard perfect and simple. The back window, a stunning oval shape, glittered in the light. A neat stack of brown leather suitcases perched above the boot.

He worked out exactly what he'd tell Theo: he'd used some of his hard-earned savings for its acquisition. Having his own transport would give him independence. He'd be able to motor to and from Charlbury as he wished, and not interfere with Theo's busy schedule.

He meant to buy it. The car would become a home from home. A place where he'd teach the beautiful Beatrice Davenport to drive. A place where they could eat and talk and laugh. A private place where they could be together …

He bent to peer intently at the mascot.

'We call her "The Spirit of Ecstasy",' said a voice behind him. 'The figurehead in her body-clinging gown. It's a new design from Rolls-Royce.'

'Oh, really?' He straightened his back. He grinned across at the hopeful salesman in his smart uniform. 'Stunning, isn't she? I've just *got* to have her. May I take her for a spin – and how much will she cost?'

'One of my distinguished neighbours,' Theo said, meticulously dabbing at his lips over the asparagus soup, 'seems to have bought himself the most beautiful little Rolls. I spotted it sitting outside the house the moment I got here.'

Alex looked intently at his brother. 'Actually, Theo, the buyer is closer to home.'

Theo stared across at him. 'Whatever do you mean?'

'It's not one of your good neighbours … it's me.'

Theo's spoon hovered in mid-air. 'I *beg* your pardon?'

'I've bought a car.' His heart skipped a proud beat. 'I need to be thoroughly independent. I went to that showroom in

150

St John's Wood you told me about. She's divine, isn't she? I'm only her second owner and she has hardly any miles on the clock.' He added bashfully, 'They gave me a very reasonable price.'

Theo looked dumbfounded. He rattled his spoon into his empty bowl. 'And what on God's *earth* did you do for *money*, dearest bro?'

Alex's proud heart skipped another beat, this time with anger.

'I have some savings. I went to the bank this morning. They gave me a cheque book for my entirely solvent account.' He lowered his eyes to stop looking at Theo whom he suddenly found he utterly detested. 'I'll have you know,' his voice choked, 'that I'm not the pathetic, incapable drunkard you assume I've become.'

Theo rose swiftly to his feet. 'Forgive me.' He walked the length of the elegant table to press his brother's hand. 'I was out of order. I didn't mean to patronise you.' He cuffed Alex gently on the side of his head. 'I'm absolutely delighted. It's just what you need. You'll be able to come and go, see something of England's glorious countryside. Take a real vacation.'

Theo returned to his chair.

'Let's eat up. Then you can show me your new baby. We can't have her sitting on our doorstep without giving her a welcome-to-your-new-owners fling, now, can we?'

Alex had spent the afternoon sitting in the Rolls, taking her for a test drive, filling out the paperwork, writing out a cheque, making sure the car was safely delivered to the correct address and then lovingly dusting her leather seats and polishing her windscreen, desperate to show his beautiful acquisition to Beatrice Davenport.

He bit his lip, took his soup bowl to the covered food

trolley and started to serve the lamb casserole that Theo's housekeeper had made for them.

'Great!' Theo picked up his fork. 'This smells wonderful. After we've eaten, we'll go for a spin in your stunning new acquisition. You can take the wheel and I'll show you London.'

Beatrice

'Are you really telling me that Emile Dubois is now my *stepfather?*' Charlotte scrunched her fingers over the crisp white hospital sheet. 'Is this some terrible joke?'

Beatrice bit her lip, trying to settle more comfortably on the cold, slippery bedside chair. She'd decided not to tell Charlotte that Miriam was about to have another baby. That piece of scintillating news could wait until her niece was safely back at Chandos.

Miriam's telegram had hit her like a thunderbolt. She'd often been jealous of her sister, but to hear that she'd been pregnant almost from the start of her liaison with Emile was devastating. Miriam and Emile could hardly have *wanted* a child, couldn't possibly have planned to have one – let alone longed for one as she and Victor had done for four interminable years. She dreaded telling Victor, but she'd have to face him with the news on Friday.

Trying to sustain her encouraging smile, she defended Emile.

'Oh, come on, darling. He's not as bad as that. He's been wonderful to your mother, protecting her from the press, looking after her in Europe, taking her to his own home, and now making her a respectable woman. He's a distinguished novelist. He could have had his pick of attractive women. He must love Miriam very much.'

'Well, he certainly loves her more than I do at the moment. When will he finish the novel he's writing and come home to Kensington?' Charlotte pushed back her hair. 'They wouldn't expect me to live with them in France, would they? Because I won't, not for a single day.'

Beatrice looked up with gratitude as a nurse brought them a tray with tea and slices of sponge cake.

'I've no idea what Miriam plans to do. But she wouldn't want to uproot you permanently.' She poured Charlotte a cup of tea. 'By the way, Laura and the girls send their love and say get better soon.'

'And you should be with them, shouldn't you? It's Wednesday afternoon, one of your working days. Instead you're sitting with me in this dreary hospital.' Charlotte's eyes filled with tears of self-pity. 'It's Rosalind's party next week. You've made me that beautiful dress. But I won't be able to go now, will I? Ros will be so upset.'

'I'm sorry, Charlotte. You're recovering splendidly. Your doctor's delighted with your progress. If all goes well, you can come back to Chandos with me next Monday … But you'll need to rest and recuperate there for at least a month.'

Charlotte stuffed an enormous slice of lemon sponge into her mouth. 'Can Dr Hertzler come to see me here before I leave?' she asked, scattering pieces of cake everywhere.

Beatrice blushed, hoping Charlotte wouldn't notice. 'I'm sure he will, darling. He's due back in Charlbury any day now. I'll let you know as soon as I hear from him.'

'He was wonderful, wasn't he? I mean, he knew exactly

what was wrong with me and he didn't make a silly fuss. He just saved my life.' Charlotte gulped her tea. 'I'd really like to thank him properly.'

Beatrice thought, You and me both. She stood up to brush at Charlotte's crumbs.

Chandos felt particularly quiet that afternoon. She got home to find that Foxie had retired to bed with a headache. Unable to settle to anything, she wandered from room to room, checking that everything was neat and tidy. Charlotte's room sparkled, ready for her return.

For an hour she walked in the garden, watched the rabbits scampering beside the river, listened to the early evening birdsong. Almost without realising where she was going, she moved down to the spot where she and Alex had talked on Saturday night. His question, so direct and unexpected, echoed in her mind.

'Aren't you ever lonely?'

She was drowning in a lake of loneliness. She missed Laura and the girls, in the world where nobody had time to stand around, thinking about themselves and mulling over their problems. Dearest Laura! Steadfast and loyal to the last, she never complained about being left in the lurch with a collection of unfinished dresses, hard-working girls and demanding clients.

Their partnership was solid as a rock. A wave of gratitude flooded her heart. She could never be lonely for long with Laura at the other end of a telephone, waiting for her return to Hampstead.

She must do something fast to fill the twilight hours. She'd write to the twins: two identical letters as always, telling them about Miriam's marriage, but focusing on their sister's brave battle with her appendix. The twins liked Emile. She hoped the news he was now their stepfather would go down better with them than it had with their sister.

Her hat on, a wrap across her shoulders and the letters in her bag, Beatrice left Chandos, crossing the narrow lane and walking through the quiet churchyard, past its massive fir tree, into Church Street.

She needed to pass Theo's cottage to reach the post box in Market Street. But she stayed on the other side of the road, pretending not to notice it. She mustn't be caught looking in the windows – although she longed to march up to the front door and ring the bell.

Was anyone at home?

It was not until she'd posted the letters and had walked back down Church Street that she noticed a small, cream-painted Rolls-Royce sitting outside Theo's. She decided to take a closer look. As she moved towards it, Theo's front door swung open.

'Good evening, Mrs Davenport,' called Alexander. 'I was just about to come knocking on your door …' He bounced down the short path and took her hand. He wore an open-neck shirt and carpet slippers. His hair, usually carefully combed away from his forehead, fell forward in wavy streaks as if it were dancing for joy.

'How do you like my new baby? How is your niece? And most important of all, how are *you*?'

A blush rose to her cheeks at the touch of his hand.

'Thank you, I'm fine, Charlotte's on the road to recovery and incredibly grateful for your help.' She turned to look at the elegant motor. 'Is this really yours?'

'Mine, all mine!' Alex opened the palm of his left hand. 'Here's my new ignition key as proof of ownership.'

'That was fast work … Congratulations.'

'Thank you! ... How do you feel about having some driving lessons?'

She gasped. 'I *beg* your pardon?'

'You told me you didn't know how to drive. So I went to London and bought this Rolls-Royce, second hand. I spent yesterday pottering around London in her, getting to know her and finding my bearings in the city. She handles beautifully: easy, smooth, obeys instructions to a fault.

'I drove myself to Charlbury in her this morning. A wonderful chance for me to see some of your magical countryside. And if you'll come with me, I can teach you how to drive.'

She looked at him, energy and excitement bursting from every word. She glanced down the street. Her neighbours were probably watching the two of them, their eyes popping out of their heads. She didn't care who saw her or what they overheard.

'What a fabulous idea.'

'Isn't it just?' Alex rocked on his slippered heels. 'One of the best I've ever had.'

She said primly, 'Of course, I'll have to ask my husband.' She wouldn't say a word to Victor about the lessons if she could possibly avoid it.

'Don't be ridiculous, Mrs Davenport.' Alex danced round to the far side of the Rolls and opened the door. 'You're your own woman, aren't you? How can he possibly object? Tell your husband his Daimler and chauffeur can return to London tomorrow to be at his beck and call. I'll drive you to the hospital to see Charlotte in my new baby, with you by my side ... Come and take a look at her. Try the seat for size. It's remarkably comfortable. She really is a perfect specimen.'

Beatrice climbed into the Rolls. It smelled of new leather

and Alexander's hair oil. It was smaller than the Daimler, more compact – and a great deal more intimate. The dashboard gleamed back at her as she looked at it for the first time.

She said, 'And there's a perfect specimen of a light supper waiting for you at Chandos if you'd care to join me in half an hour … Without your carpet slippers, Dr Hertzler.'

'Thank you *so* much, Mrs Davenport.' Alex turned to smile at her, his grey eyes sparkling with anticipation and laughter. 'I see I'm not the only one around here who has good ideas.'

They lingered over coffee, sitting near the conservatory in the warmth of the garden, reluctant to end the evening.

Alex filled a pause. 'I wanted to tell you … Charlotte's appendicitis … There's something about the condition that's particularly special for me.'

'Have you ever performed the operation?'

'I have, several times at St Luke's. But what makes it special is that it's the first operation I ever watched my father carry out. It was my sixteenth birthday. I knew I wanted to be a doctor, just like him and Theo and Grandpa.

'Pa promised to take me on his rounds for the day. He warned me it was going to be rough and tough, and that I must never talk about the details to anyone.

'We had a horse called Dobbin and an old buggy we used every day. Pa fell asleep for most of the journey, but Dobbin knew exactly where to go. The Kansas prairie stretched for miles, with nothing in sight but bunch-grass and thistles. The family we were visiting were dirt poor. Pa had no hope of ever getting paid, but he didn't care. When his patients needed him, he went, come hell or high water.

'We reached a dark, crumpled-looking two-room shack. Inside was an old stove, a table and a few boxes for chairs. Lying on a rough-looking bed in the corner was a girl, crouched double over her stomach, groaning in agony.

'Pa examined her, said, "Appendicitis," and operated immediately.

'I just stood there open-mouthed, watching him handle the sharp knife, the pale body, the dark blood. He was so swift and confident. I was full of admiration.

'Afterwards, when it was all over – the table cleaned, the floor mopped, the girl sleeping peacefully – her parents put a few coins into Pa's hand. He smiled, shook his head and gave them the money back. I'll never forget the look of gratitude in their eyes.

'As we climbed back on the buggy, Pa told me we'd been just in time. Another few hours and the girl would have died of peritonitis. The whole day, the excitement of it, my Pa's dedication – I can remember it as vividly as if it had happened yesterday.'

'And you'll return to your New York hospital at the end of your sabbatical?'

Alex looked across at her for a long moment.

'I guess I'll have to. At least I'm useful there. On a good day, the sense of satisfaction is heart-warming and marvellous. Besides, I don't know any other life.' He pushed back his chair and stood up, holding out his hand. 'Thank you for another lovely evening. I'll be outside your door at eleven tomorrow morning, and you can start your great adventure. Freedom and independence, here we come.'

'I can hardly wait.' She imagined sitting behind the wheel of the Rolls, the Oxfordshire fields either side, and Alex sitting next to her, as companion and guide. 'Have you decided where we'll go?'

'I've been looking at Theo's map. One of your nearest villages is Stonesfield. I suggest I drive there. You can watch everything I do and I'll talk you through the technical details. Then you can take over, for say twenty minutes.'

Anticipation and fear flooded her body.

They walked back into Chandos and stood together at the front door.

He asked, 'Shall we give our car a name?'

She opened the door, shivering at the sudden gust of cool air.

'How about Hermione? Graceful, elegant, smooth.'

'Perfect. I love it ... Sleep well, Beatrice. I'm off to say good night to Hermione.'

Charlotte

On Monday the 15th of May, Betty, the day nurse who'd looked after Charlotte for a week, bustled into her room.

Charlotte sat by the window in the summer suit Auntie Bea had brought in. After wearing her floppy, full-skirted nightdress for what seemed like months, her underwear and clothes felt strange and uncomfortable.

'You'll be delighted to hear your doctor has given you the all clear.' Betty put a cup of coffee on the bedside table and tweaked at the blanket. 'Mrs Davenport has just telephoned. She'll be collecting you this afternoon at three.'

Charlotte sighed with relief. 'Thank goodness!' She glanced across the room. 'Sorry, Betty. That sounds awful … You've been wonderful, you all have, you've looked after me so well, but – '

'You'll be glad to get home.'

'I can hardly wait. My tummy still feels sore and I can't walk very fast, but that ghastly pain has completely disappeared.'

'You take good care of yourself over the next few weeks. If you feel tired, stop what you're doing immediately and

161

rest.' Betty dug her hand into her starched apron pocket. 'I nearly forgot … This letter arrived for you, just in time.'

She recognised the writing in an instant, feeling dizzy with surprise.

'If anything else arrives for you after you've left, I'll make sure it's sent on to you in Charlbury. Don't let your coffee go cold.'

She tore at the envelope. It smelled of antiseptic.

London   *Saturday 13 May 1911*

My dearest Charlotte

I am sure you will be astonished to hear from me again, but I had to write to you one more time. I was at a party last night, and who should I meet there but your best friend Rosalind. She told me you were in the Radcliffe, and why. I was so upset to hear the news, and hope with all my heart you have thoroughly recovered – and indeed that this letter reaches you before you leave.

I also wanted to apologise for my mother's monstrous behaviour towards you. I am sure I put your letters in the safest place in my room, and I have no idea how she found them lying on my bed. She has kept her discovery a secret from my father, but only on condition that I stopped seeing you. She was so furious about the whole affair that I had no choice but to go along with her wishes.

Needless to say, I miss you very much. My Wednesday afternoons are now totally consumed with work. I have to take a load of exams next month, but when I am not thinking about them, I am thinking of you.

You are a brilliant girl: beautiful, intelligent and so understanding. It is with the deepest of regrets that I shall not be able to meet with you again.

Your loving friend
Sebastian

She stood up to grab her coffee and gulp it down, her hand shaking, her heart pounding with anger, with resentment. And questions.

Why had it taken Sebastian so long to write her a letter of apology? What exactly had Rosalind told him? Whose party had Rosalind and Sebastian been at? She should have been there too, in London, with her friends, eating and drinking and dancing to the latest fashionable tunes, not stuck in a hospital bed as if she were ninety-four and counting.

She read the letter for a second time and then a third, knowing it said too little and had come much too late. Presumably if Sebastian hadn't suddenly realised she might be at death's door, she'd never have heard from him again. She made herself tear the letter into shreds and chuck it in the bin.

Back in her chair by the window she remembered that ghastly afternoon, when she'd watched Lady Manners climb into her cab and disappear. How the cruelty of her words had pounded their way round and round her head. How humiliated and desperate she'd felt, not knowing what to do or where to go.

In the end she'd gone to see Rosalind, who was thankfully at home and on her own. She'd poured out her heart to her, unable to stem the tears – or to forgive Sebastian for not arriving himself that afternoon to tell her, face to face, they couldn't meet again.

The pain wouldn't have been any less, but at least she could have talked to him for the last time, given him the tie-pin as his Easter gift – and finally, perhaps, done what she'd so often dreamed of doing: kissing him, even if it were only to say goodbye.

During the weeks that followed she went to bed to sob silently into her pillow, took long lonely walks by herself in Charlbury's fields, spent several Wednesday afternoons just before and after Easter with Rosalind, did her best to talk to the twins without revealing her misery, and decided one thing for absolute certainty.

She'd never allow herself to fall in love again. Although she had no idea exactly how, she'd plan a life for herself as an independent woman, with a proper career that gave her freedom and purpose. She'd build her own good name and reputation. Nobody would ever be able to humiliate her as Lady Manners had done with those few devastating words.

When Auntie Bea arrived with Dr Hertzler on the dot of three, she'd already packed her small suitcase and was burning with impatience. They walked slowly out to the cars parked at the front of the hospital.

Her aunt said gaily, 'Guess which one we'll be going home in.'

She searched for but couldn't find the Daimler. 'I've no idea.'

'Here.' Auntie Bea drew her towards a cream-painted Rolls. 'This is Dr Hertzler's latest acquisition. We call it Hermione.' She gave her niece a brief hug. 'I've had two driving lessons in her and she handles like a dream.'

'I thought you were looking happier than usual.'

Her aunt laughed. She helped her climb into the back seat. 'Of course, you're not to tell your uncle. He'll accuse me of gallivanting around the countryside without his express permission.'

'As a matter of fact,' Dr Hertzler settled himself behind the wheel, 'your aunt is a natural driver. She wasn't a bit nervous. Within the space of twenty minutes, she'd taken to the road as if she owned it.'

Auntie Bea glanced at him under the brim of her hat. She had a soft radiance about her that Charlotte had never noticed before.

'Actually, my stomach was churning with terror for the first ten minutes, but I hoped you wouldn't notice! You're a very good driving instructor. You showed me what I needed to know, you made it look simple, and you gave me confidence.'

Dr Hertzler swung Hermione on to the Woodstock Road.

'Great,' he said. 'If I ever decide to give up being a doctor, I know exactly what my new career will be.'

Later that afternoon, after they'd had tea on the lawn and Dr Hertzler had left for Theo's cottage, Auntie Bea took her upstairs to unpack.

'I have to go to London on Wednesday. Laura has been wonderful. She managed without me all last week with never a murmur. But it's much too soon for you to spend hours on the train, and then fighting London traffic. Will you be all right here with Foxie?'

'Of course.' She perched on her bed. The last place she wanted to be was London, where all her friends were being presented at Court and meeting Sebastian at parties. 'It's lovely to be back. Thank you for letting me stay here.'

'It's a pleasure to have you.' Auntie Bea hung one of her dresses in the wardrobe. 'Dr Hertzler says he'll come to have tea with you every afternoon. You can play cards and talk medicine and walk in the garden. The weather's been perfect lately. Would you like that, darling?'

She remembered the touch of Dr Hertzler's hand as he helped her out of the car. The way his dark hair fell over his forehead when he laughed. The sound of his deep voice with its seductive American twang.

'Oh, yes, Auntie Bea,' she said. 'I'd like that very much indeed.'

Charlotte fell into a deep and dreamless sleep, back in her own bed again that night. Foxie told her she'd be excused lessons for the whole week, so instead she read novels, walked slowly in the garden – and waited patiently for Dr Hertzler's afternoon arrival.

'In a few weeks' time you'll be able to move more easily,' he said. 'I see you have a tennis court over there behind the stables. We can play a few gentle games as soon as you feel like it.'

'I could make you a new tennis skirt and blouse.' Auntie Bea poured their tea.

'And tomorrow, while your aunt is in London,' Dr Hertzler looked at Beatrice over his cup, 'I could take you for a short spin in Hermione.'

'I'd love that.'

'By the way, Charlotte, please call me Alex. All this Dr Hertzler stuff makes me feel uncomfortable.'

'You're a very lucky girl,' Auntie Bea said. 'While I'm slaving over my dress designs and London clients, you'll have the wind in your hair and Alex at the wheel.'

'But I hope to have *you* behind the wheel next Monday.' Alex gave Beatrice a sparkling smile. 'You may be an excellent beginner, but only practice makes perfect.'

'And in return, you must ride Victor's horses,' Auntie Bea said. 'You can come as early as you like, through the side gate into the garden, and not disturb anyone. Victor will be so grateful. The horses love the exercise. Our groom can show you which one needs you the most. You can ride each of them in turn.'

The rest of that week went perfectly according to plan. Under the early summer sun, afternoons with Alex turned Charlotte's dull recovery into an adventure. She discovered for the first time what fun it was to spend time alone with a man who was not her father or a secret liaison – but who was fast becoming a real friend.

Auntie Bea and Uncle Victor arrived at Chandos on Friday evening. On Saturday Victor rode a couple of his horses early, then disappeared to spend the day fishing by the river. He returned at six o'clock. Charlotte sat in the conservatory with her aunt, watching her sketch some new designs for the winter season.

Uncle Victor stood in the doorway, his face flushed.

'I managed to catch a couple of trout … We can have them for supper.'

'Congratulations.' Auntie Bea looked up from her work. 'So you had a peaceful and successful day.'

'Very successful indeed but hardly peaceful … One of my chums, who's also a fisherman, told me all about what you've been getting up to.'

Auntie Bea put down her pencils. 'I *beg* your pardon?'

'Too right you do! I gather you've been seen driving around the village with that Hertzler fellow.'

'If you mean Alexander, then, yes, your fisherman friend is quite correct. Alex has been giving me driving lessons.'

'What on earth for? You've got my chauffeur and the Daimler if you need to go anywhere.'

'But you need them too. Being able to drive will be incredibly useful. I might even buy myself a car. And Alex has been marvellous. He's a brilliant instructor. He's spent a lot of time and patience not only teaching me, but driving Charlotte home from hospital, having tea with her every afternoon, helping her to recover from her operation.'

'The fellow must be a real goody two-shoes! I wonder what else he can do for you!'

'Don't be obscene, Victor.' Auntie Bea stood up, scattering her drawings to the floor. 'Kindly stop behaving like a child, especially in front of Charlotte ... If you must know, Alex has also been riding your horses for you every morning, and doing you and your groom a real favour. If you've got any more complaints about him, I'd be grateful if you kept them to yourself ... Those fish are starting to smell. Take them to Cook. Ask her to grill them for us tonight.'

Charlotte waited until her uncle had stormed off to the kitchen. Then she followed her aunt upstairs.

'Do you want me to ask Alex not to come to tea again?' She hovered at Beatrice's bedroom door.

Auntie Bea turned to look at her. 'You enjoy his company, don't you?'

Charlotte quailed at the fury that still etched her aunt's pale face. 'Of course. Very much indeed. Chandos can be a pretty lonely place when you're not here.'

'Then you have my permission to go on seeing him ... Take no notice of your uncle. Charlbury calls itself a market town. In reality it's a small village always rife with malicious gossip.'

Auntie Bea pulled two dresses from her wardrobe, shaking them out as if she wished they were her so-called neighbours.

'Victor can sometimes be incredibly petty and small-minded. He made a dreadful fuss when Alex and I rushed you to hospital without him.'

'I'm so sorry!' She frowned. 'I'd no idea he'd taken it out on you.'

Her aunt chose one of the dresses, put the other one back in the wardrobe and slammed the door.

'Go and change for dinner, darling. We'll both look as presentable as possible and talk about the things that really matter.'

But their meal was a miserable affair. Uncle Victor refused to apologise. He sat hunched and sulky in his chair, looking as if he'd much rather be drinking in the pub.

When Auntie Bea mentioned the celebrations at Eton that were, as always, planned for the Fourth of June, he asked her abruptly why 'that sister of yours' couldn't be there for the twins. He then told her grumpily he supposed he'd have to give up a Sunday to drive her and Charlotte to Windsor.

'It'll be fun, Victor,' Auntie Bea said. 'We'll take a delicious picnic, and watch the boys playing cricket. They go on the river, standing up in their boats with flowers in their hats. It's the most important day in the Eton calendar. It marks the birthday of King George III. The twins are expecting us to be there. We're all they've got.'

Uncle Victor pushed an enormous slice of fish into his mouth and started to chew.

The days of June continued to be filled with sunshine. Charlotte felt physically better every day, although she worried about her aunt. It was a relief every Monday morning when her uncle left Chandos in his Daimler and they had the place to themselves.

Alex had quickly become a crucial part of her life – but it was not until the end of the month that she realised just how important.

It was a Monday morning. She'd had lessons with Foxie, and came downstairs for lunch to find her aunt sitting in the conservatory, a letter lying in her lap, her face wet with tears.

'Whatever's the matter?' She knelt beside her. 'You've

been crying.' She glanced down at the letter. 'Is that from Miriam? … It's not bad news, is it?'

'Yes and no.' Auntie Bea took out a handkerchief. 'I couldn't tell you sooner in case it all went wrong.' She looked down at her and stroked her hair. 'Your mother has had another baby. A little girl. They've called her Violet.'

'*What?*'

'That's the good news, I suppose, although it's very hard for me. I so long to have a child and Miriam's not exactly the world's best mother.'

'You can say that again.' Charlotte felt as if the air had been sucked from her lungs. 'Is that why she's stayed away all this time? She might have had the decency to tell *me*.'

'She only told *me* because your uncle sent her a cable after you'd been taken to hospital. It gave her a cast-iron excuse for not travelling to your bedside.'

'I see.' Charlotte's head began to buzz with worry. 'And the bad news?'

'The bad news,' Auntie Bea said slowly, as if the words were forcing themselves out of her mouth in hard pellets of reluctance and gloom, 'the bad news is that Miriam and Emile will be travelling back to Kensington in a fortnight. They want the twins to go there directly from Eton at the end of term … and you're to join them.'

Charlotte stood up, her legs trembling, her mouth dry as dust. 'I'm not leaving you, Auntie Bea. Not after all these months. Don't make me.'

'I'm so sorry, darling. It breaks my heart to send you back to Miriam. But you're *her* daughter and I don't have any choice.'

'I don't want lunch.' Charlotte ran out of the conservatory, through the hall, upstairs to the sanctuary of her room.

The full-summer garden basked in the midday sun. The

tinder-dry lawn was already tinged with gold. In a couple of hours, Alex would be sitting out there with her. Did she really now have to count the few remaining afternoons during which they could be together?

Before Easter she'd vowed she'd never fall in love again. Now she knew it wasn't something you could choose. It had happened to her for a second time in one enormous passionate tidal wave – and she was floundering beneath it.

Beatrice

By the middle of June, she knew she'd learned to drive. She recognised the purring sound of Hermione's engine. She could use hand signals to tell other drivers where she intended to go. On narrow country lanes, she knew how to deal with oncoming tractors, and farmers with their shire horses and enormous carts, without swerving into the nearest ditch.

She understood the language of road signs, which she'd never needed to look at before. She began to love the tiny hamlets that lay along their path as she and Alex made their short journeys of discovery.

They were never out for more than two hours. She'd pack a small basket of cakes and lemonade. She'd be ready and waiting for Alex on Chandos's drive. They'd consult his map and decide where new to go. They'd drive for an hour, stop for coffee or drink the lemonade, and motor back to Charlbury, taking the driving in turns from start to finish.

One morning they drove through Spelsbury to Chipping Norton, where Alex shopped for food: Theo's housekeeper was on holiday and he had to fend for himself. One particularly hot day, they chose Leafield, sitting on the grass by the side of the Church of St Michael and All Angels. It gave them welcome peace and shade.

She was amazed at how quickly this ritual of Monday and Tuesday mornings became part of her Chandos life – and how crucial to her the man who sat beside her grew to be.

They could talk about anything. They shared a sense of fun. She often returned to Chandos, her stomach aching with laughter. Alex was always in her thoughts as she took the train to London on Wednesday mornings; as she worked on her new designs with Laura beside her; as she ate dinner with Victor in St John's Wood.

When the Coronation took place on a damp morning in London on the 22nd of June, she and Laura took the girls to watch the royal procession in the crowded streets. In spite of the excitement, the cheering, and the waving flags, all she could think about was whether Alex and Charlotte were enjoying their street party in Charlbury.

One morning towards the end of June, they drove through Stonesfield and Combe to Woodstock. She wanted to show Alex the beauty of the Blenheim Palace gardens. In Woodstock, they left Hermione in Park Street and walked through Blenheim's Admiralty Arch gate. Beneath a sky of Italian blue, they stood looking at the outline of the Palace, the glorious lake and the picture postcard bridge.

'Wow!' Alex sucked in his breath. 'That sure is one of the most beautiful sights I've ever seen.'

'We can walk round the lake to Rosamond's Well. It'll be cooler there under the trees.'

Half an hour later, they drank lemonade as seagulls swooped low over the water and a couple of squirrels stopped to inspect them near the edge of the lake.

'There's something I've always meant to ask you.' Alex sat beside her on the grass with his legs bent, his arms resting on them, a glass in his hand. 'You and Victor are such an odd match. Wasn't there anyone in your life before you met him, someone you loved and could have married?'

She blushed. 'There was, of course. I didn't meet Victor until I was twenty-five. But I never talk about the great love of my young life.'

'You can talk to me, can't you?'

She took a deep breath, knowing she could. 'His name was Ralph Brightman. He was Laura's brother and a brilliant photographer. I met him soon after I met Laura. And yes, before you ask, it was love at first sight … for us both.'

'So what happened?'

'The worst night of my life.'

'Tell me about it … the whole story.'

'You're sure you want to hear it?'

Alex turned to look at her, his grey eyes flickering with passion. 'Quite sure.'

'Well, then, here goes … Laura and I met while we were at The Slade. It's an art school in London. We became firm friends. Ralph was already established as a photographer. He was an extraordinary person: he moved like quicksilver. He did everything fast: he walked fast, talked fast, made rapid decisions. He saw the world in a series of dazzling snapshots. After I'd spent three evenings with him, I felt I'd known him all my life.'

'It's a question of chemistry.'

'Exactly. It was like meeting a kindred spirit. I loved being in his Chelsea studio, watching him work. He was brilliant with people. He always managed to produce an image that was unexpected, honest and absolutely unique.'

'So what happened?'

'We first met in the autumn term. By June the following summer, he asked me to marry him. The following six months were some of the happiest of my life. My father and Ralph adored each other, and the four of us – Laura, Ralph, my father and I – used to meet every Friday night for supper, come what may.

'At the end of that year, it was almost Christmas, Laura and I had planned to go to a party at The Slade with Ralph. The weather was vile: bitterly cold and foggy. As the day wore on, the fog got much worse.

'By the time evening fell, you could hardly see your nose in front of your face. Laura and I were waiting for Ralph to pick us up from Hampstead and take us to the party. We waited and waited …

'Midnight came. Two in the morning. Laura took a cab back to Chelsea. We both sat up all night for Ralph but he never arrived.'

Her hand shaking, she poured herself another glass of lemonade.

'Twenty-four hours later, the police arrived. Ralph had been killed. They asked us to identify his body.' She paused. 'We tried to piece together the fragments of what we think must have happened.

'Ralph had been in Fleet Street for a meeting with the editor of a fashion magazine. A group of men were coming out of a nearby pub, locked in a drunken brawl. Ralph may or may not have attempted to break it up. We'll never know the details.

'In any event, someone punched him, either deliberately or by mistake. The blow sent him staggering into the road, where he was hit by a cab. All the other men who were involved fled the scene. There was only one witness. He saw very little, and the fog made everything worse.

'Laura was devastated, I was heartbroken … and my father never recovered. He died of pneumonia three months later. I had to get on with my life without him *and* without Ralph. Almost too much to bear.'

'How did you survive?'

'We worked through it.' Her voice trembled. 'Laura and I finished our course at The Slade and we set up our dressmaking business together. It became our salvation.

'She sold the house she'd shared with Ralph in Chelsea and moved to be my next-door neighbour in Hampstead. Thank God for *A Passion for Fashion*. It's our own small enterprise. Nobody can take it away from us.'

For the first time, Alex reached across to her. He took her hand and raised it briefly to his lips.

'I did the same. I coped with death by flinging myself at my job in St Luke's and practically working *myself* to death.' He let her hand fall to her lap and turned his head away, as if he wanted to add something. But he changed his mind.

Instead, he murmured, 'It's the only way … You *have* to go forward, come what may. And then, one morning you wake up and – God knows how – you know you've crossed the river.'

They walked back to Woodstock under the blazing midday sun in silence – and deep companionship.

'Won't you come to London with me?' Victor asked that Monday morning at the beginning of July. 'Now that Charlotte and Foxie have disappeared, there's nobody to keep you here.'

'I'd prefer to stay,' she said quickly. 'I need to do some housekeeping. I'm not dressed for town and it's going to be another sweltering day.'

Victor kissed her forehead, his moustache prickling against her skin.

'Very well, dear. If you're out in the garden, stay in the shade and drink plenty of water.'

'Just like your horses, eh, Victor?'

He grunted with laughter. 'See you as usual on Wednesday. We've got the Skinners coming for supper, remember? I need you to look your best.'

She almost said, 'I always look my best for you, Victor.' Then she glanced down at the skimpy muslin frock she'd flung on for breakfast with her husband, and decided against.

The Daimler puffed out of the drive. She climbed the stairs to her bedroom, listening to the haunting silence. She missed the hum of voices that usually came from Foxie and Charlotte in the school room.

She remembered sitting with them both last Wednesday on the train to Paddington: the tears on Charlotte's pale cheeks, Foxie's lips clamped together. The devastating moments when she'd put them and their suitcases in a cab bound for Kensington, watching Charlotte frantically waving goodbye through the cab window, wondering when she'd see them again – and turning away to face another busy working day with Laura and the girls.

Miriam had telephoned her in Hampstead.

'Everybody's arrived safely.' Her voice trembled with happiness. 'All my family are together again ... Thank you *so* much for looking after Charlotte for me ... Our baby Violet's an absolute angel. She's got Emile's wonderful hazel eyes and he simply *dotes* on her. She's just beginning to sleep through the night ... You *must* come and meet her very soon.'

But on Friday morning a second call followed.

'I've just hired a nanny for Violet,' Miriam told her. 'The

weather in London is so hot at the moment, we've decided to go down to St Ives next week for the rest of the summer. You and Victor are welcome to join us. Emile says you'd be our guests, our way of trying to return your very generous hospitality.'

Beatrice managed to say, 'Thank you, Miriam, but we're both much too busy at the moment,' before she put down the receiver, burning with a jealousy that threatened to consume her soul.

She had two hours to kill before Alex's arrival. She checked that Charlotte's room stood empty and clean; Foxie had left her own bedroom spotless. She'd tidy her wardrobe, spend half an hour pulling out some frocks that needed washing, their hems mending, their lace collars given special ironing.

She wandered into Victor's dressing room and opened his wardrobe. Hanging on the rail was a green velvet smoking jacket that looked brand new. She wondered whether she'd ever seen him wearing it.

As she pulled it off its hanger to examine it, the faint but unmistakable scent of hyacinths rose into the air. She dug her hand through its pockets. The two on the outside of the jacket were empty. In the inside pocket, Beatrice pulled out a small white lace handkerchief. In one of its corners, carefully embroidered in purple thread, were the initials *MK*.

She started to shake with indignation and fury. She crushed the piece of lace in her hand. The scent of hyacinths grew stronger, as if it were mocking her.

Who on earth did the handkerchief belong to? She racked her memory for the names of the women she knew. None of them owned those initials. Had Victor taken a mistress in London? Where had he met her? Who was she? She assumed they must have been to bed together. You don't put someone's perfumed lace handkerchief in your pocket unless you're on the most intimate of terms ...

And then she asked herself whether she really cared.

She perched on Victor's bed. She couldn't remember when they'd last made love. Perhaps it was hardly surprising if Victor had taken up with a mistress. For the first time she admitted she too had found somebody else.

The difference was that in all the summer weeks she'd known Alex, she'd never for a single moment allowed herself to step out of line. That morning in Blenheim, beside the lake, when Alex had kissed her hand: that had been the first time – apart from their initial formal handshake – that they'd properly touched each other.

How many times had she longed to fold herself in his arms, kiss him, admit her feelings, listen to his own words of love? But she'd kept her distance, carefully and with the utmost difficulty, over and over again.

Furious and humiliated, Beatrice stuffed the handkerchief back into Victor's jacket and flung it on its rail. To rid herself of the scent of hyacinths, she took a long, cool bath and washed her hair. She asked Cook to prepare a full picnic lunch for two, not just cakes and lemonade.

She dressed carefully in a long turquoise skirt and white blouse. At five minutes to eleven, she tied on a huge white picture hat and slid on a pair of white cotton gloves.

She carried the picnic basket out to the drive.

She bent to look at Alex as he drove Hermione through the gate.

'I thought we could go to Wolvercote. It's a small village just before you get to Oxford. I've packed us a delicious picnic. There's a bathing place by the river. You can swim if it's not too crowded and there's enough water in the Thames to get you properly wet.'

Alex looked at her, his dark eyelashes fluttering over his smiling grey eyes. 'In that case I'd better drive back to Theo's and collect my bathing suit. I'll wear it underneath my trousers.'

She put the basket on the back seat. She climbed into Hermione. She could smell the scent of the leather seats, the fragrance of cold chicken sandwiches, the cologne Alex had dabbed on his wrists.

'By the way,' he said. 'I really adore your hat.'

Alexander

Alex drove slowly and carefully into Charlbury for the first time on his own, and parked his Rolls-Royce outside Theo's cottage.

It had been a long drive. He was tired, dusty and famished. As the miles on the clock rose, the confidence and ebullience he'd felt over the previous few days he'd spent in London began to evaporate.

What on earth had he done? Spent a small fortune on a car he could only just afford? Committed himself to living on his own in a strange village in which he knew nobody? Become obsessed with a crazy idea that might never work? Assumed that the beautiful Beatrice would be remotely interested in meeting him again?

She belonged to another man. She had a life of her own, houses to organise, a business in London, a convalescent niece. For the space of a long and unexpectedly marvellous night he'd managed to become her hero of the hour. She'd been desperate and vulnerable. He'd been with her, by her side, throughout her ordeal.

But any local doctor who'd been summoned to

Charlotte's emergency bedside would have made the same diagnosis. He, Dr Alexander Hertzler, had only done his job. He'd been lucky enough to be at the right place, at exactly the right time.

He might never get lucky again.

He climbed out of the car, his back stiff, his bones aching. He dragged his suitcase along the short path and opened the cottage door. He slammed it behind him, and breathed a sigh of relief. He had no idea what he wanted to happen over the coming summer months, but hey, he was here, in one piece, waiting and ready. Nothing ventured, nothing gained ...

The cottage was scrupulously tidy. The housekeeper, who came several mornings a week, had responded to Theo's letter of instructions and left fresh bread, cheese, ham and a bowl of summer fruit in the pantry.

He made himself an enormous tea, unpacked his suitcase, took a bath, flung on a pair of clean trousers and an open-necked shirt. He hovered in the front sitting room, glancing out of the window every now and then, trying to summon up the courage to call at Chandos.

Which is when he saw Beatrice on the other side of the road, walking into the village. His heart in his mouth, he waited by the window until he saw her return. Then he flung himself out of the door.

When, much later, he looked back on those days of May and June, he remembered them as glittering charms on a never-ending necklace of golden summer days.

Every weekday, just after dawn, he'd throw on his riding clothes and walk to Chandos. He rode each of the three geldings and then the mare in turn, trotting them through the dew-filled garden down to the river and beyond, to the quietly rustling fields and the woods of Cornbury Park.

He'd return to Theo's cottage, take a bath, eat breakfast. On Mondays and Tuesdays he'd wait impatiently until it was time for his date with Beatrice at eleven. He'd eat lunch on his own, sleep for an hour and take tea with Charlotte and Beatrice back at Chandos. In the evenings he read Theo's medical books and journals, or pottered around the walled garden, tidying, sweeping, pruning.

The weekends were different.

On Saturdays and Sundays he let Victor and Theo take over the horses, deliberately avoiding Victor, not wanting to interfere with Theo's relationship with his neighbourhood friends. He walked in the village, took the car out on his own to the surrounding villages – and waited until the moment when he could, once again, spend time with Beatrice.

He was head over heels in love. He'd never experienced the cascade of feelings that flooded through him when they were together. And he had time on his hands in which to savour the moment.

When he'd met Lillian and fallen in love with her, he was already working at St Luke's. Their relationship had been constantly dominated by his medical schedules, his need to sleep after days of relentless hospital duty, their preparations for their wedding, finding a house they both liked and that her parents agreed to buy. The whole frenetic hubbub of New York life.

The hours he spent with Beatrice seemed to hang in a precious, specially created universe that only existed for the two of them, outside the humdrum demands of ordinary life.

Throughout those weeks, he behaved impeccably. He taught her to drive, sat with her in the cool quiet corners they found in the countryside, drank her lemonade, took tea with her niece, rode her husband's horses, teased her, laughed with her, and talked endlessly about everything. All this without once touching her …

Well, only once. The story of her love affair with Ralph had so many echoes of his own life that without thinking he'd reached out to kiss her hand – and almost but not quite told her about Lillian and the fact that his wife was still alive, continuing to write to him from her European travels. Theo brought the mail with him from London: postcards from Len, bank statements, newsletters from St Luke's. Cards from Lillian, damp from their sea voyages, curling around the edges.

His feelings of guilt that he'd still not told Beatrice about his living, breathing wife mounted as the summer wore on. But the more dishonourable he felt about that, the more honourably he behaved towards the new love of his life. They were doing nothing wrong. Nothing, that is, that anyone could see.

Afterwards, in the car driving back to Chandos from Woodstock, he still felt her hand against his lips, smelled the scent she wore of lily-of-the-valley – and longed to touch her again.

He also knew it couldn't last.

Sooner or later, their magical summer spell would be broken.

That Monday morning when she'd suggested they drive to Wolvercote, he thought she looked different. A kind of wildness hovered around her that he'd never seen before. She'd obviously dressed with the most exquisite care, but beneath the professional attention to detail lurked something which said: I don't care what happens next. Let's go somewhere different. Let's spend not just two hours together, but all day.

And all night?

Hard as he tried, he couldn't stop himself wondering.

He knew that Beatrice was on her own at Chandos. Victor had driven to the City. Charlotte had taken the train to Kensington, tears in her eyes last week as she'd given him a small box.

'Thank you so much for looking after me.'

Inside lay a beautiful tie-pin. He'd blushed. He hardly deserved it. He'd only spent time with Charlotte to be near Beatrice, remain in her good books.

Beatrice was unusually silent as they drove to Wolvercote. He glanced at her from time to time from behind the wheel. As they got closer to Oxford, he asked, 'Is anything the matter?'

'It's only Victor. He's been getting on my nerves.'

'You've never complained about him before.'

'I'm supposed to be discreet and loyal, aren't I?' Beatrice sounded bitter. 'He kept telling me all weekend how wonderful it was to have Chandos to ourselves. He spent most of his time fishing or riding, so he's no idea what it's like. The empty silence …

'The fact is, I loved having Charlotte and Foxie with me, and the twins too when they came home from Eton. It's what large houses are for … Heaven only knows what he'll be like when we have children of our own.

'But then I can't have children, can I?' She swallowed a sob. 'And there's an end to it.'

'Is that all? There's something else, isn't there?'

'My God, you're very perceptive, Dr Hertzler.'

'There's another chink in your armour.'

'I found a lace handkerchief in one of Victor's jackets. It stank of hyacinths. When I first began to spend more time in Charlbury without him, Miriam warned me he'd start to play the field. I didn't believe her.'

'And now you do?'

Beatrice shifted in her seat, twisting her legs beneath her long skirt, adjusting her fabulous hat. 'The trouble is I neither know nor care. I should feel waves of passionate jealousy. I should want to be the only woman in his life … But I don't.'

Alex remembered seeing Victor in London outside the bank, his arm flung protectively around a woman who was not his wife.

He said, 'Your husband is a total idiot.'

But he did not tell Beatrice what he'd seen.

At the bathing place, groups of families sat sprawled on the grass, eating and talking beside the river.

They found a spot slightly away from the voices and laughter, spread out a rug and placed the picnic basket beneath the shade of a tree.

Alex pulled off his shirt and trousers to reveal a black swim suit with a tunic top and trunks that covered his thighs. He swam briefly in the river and returned to sit by Beatrice. She threw his towel over his shoulders.

He said, 'It's so hot I'll probably steam dry in five minutes flat.'

Two more groups of people joined the bathing place. He glanced across at them. Two more families with seven or eight small children. He noticed how Beatrice looked at them too, naked envy glittering in her eyes.

They ate their picnic and packed the plates away. Beatrice lay back on the rug, a small pillow beneath her head. He remained sitting, looking down at her as she closed her eyes. The voices and laughter on the river bank grew louder. Some of the children were swimming in the river with their father. He raised his head to watch.

And then he saw her. A little girl in a blue cotton frock. She'd trotted away from the group and was making her deliberate way towards the road – and directly into the path of an enormous farmer's cart.

One word, one name, thundered through his heart into his mouth.

He yelled, '*Sylvia!*'

He leaped to his feet. He seemed to fly across the grass and into the road. He wrapped his arms around the child, pulling her towards him as the cart clattered past. Then he lost his footing. He fell over, the child in his arms, and crashed on to the stones of the narrow pathway leading to the river.

In an instant, the child's mother was beside him, sobbing her gratitude, taking the little girl from him, wiping at her frightened tears. Blood streamed down the side of Alex's forehead. He'd cut the skin on his left leg too and his left ankle grumbled when he put his weight on it.

Beatrice stumbled towards him from the river bank.

'What happened? I shut my eyes for a single moment. When I opened them you'd disappeared.'

He took her arm and hobbled back to their rug. 'The little girl … She's the spitting image of my daughter … I looked across at her and suddenly realised she was making for the road. She'd have gone under the wheels of the cart. She'd have been …'

'Thank God you got there in time.' Beatrice pulled off

her hat. She tore at its white ribbon. 'This will make a passable bandage until I can get you home.'

They sat in Theo's kitchen, Beatrice without her hat, him still only in his swim suit. Blood from his grazed forehead dripped on his shoulder. Beatrice filled a bowl with warm water. She found a clean cloth and some antiseptic ointment.

'Are you in pain?'

'My head feels sore and my ankle aches.' He felt the relief of the damp cloth as Beatrice gently wiped his wounds. 'But I'll live to tell the tale.'

He watched her squeeze the stained water from the cloth. He felt the sting of the ointment on her fingers smoothing his skin. He noticed the flush staining her cheeks. Her hair had partly fallen in corn-gold curls down the nape of her neck.

She moved away from him to pour the bowl of water into the sink.

He said, 'Beatrice Davenport ...'

She stopped what she was doing but did not turn to face him.

'If you don't let me kiss you right this very minute,' he said quietly, 'I shall die here and now of longing and starvation.'

'Well, then, Alexander Hertzler.'

Beatrice's voice shook with love.

'You'd better take me upstairs to your bed this very minute before I have your death on my hands.'

Beatrice

Beatrice left Theo's cottage, filled with a wild, defiant joy.
At the bottom of the path she turned to wave. Alex stood
by the front window in his dressing gown. He waved back.

She opened Hermione's door to remove her hat, her
gloves and the picnic basket. She left Alex's shirt and
trousers on the back seat. She knew she was under village
scrutiny. A whole posse of Victor's fishermen friends were
watching her every move. She no longer cared. If Victor
challenged her, if he dared to object to anything she did,
she'd face him with the scented handkerchief. That would
suck the wind out of his righteous sails.

Her hair tumbling around her shoulders, she marched
through the churchyard and into Church Lane. Back in
Chandos, she gave their startled Cook the picnic basket, told
her the food had been delicious and asked for similar fare
for the following day.

She climbed the stairs to bath and change. Her skirt and
blouse were spattered with Alex's blood. Her underwear was
damp and crumpled. She stripped off her clothes in front
of her bedroom mirror, staring at her naked body as if she'd

never seen it before. It felt different. It looked different.

It now belonged to Alex.

She belonged to him.

She started to count the hours until midnight when, swiftly and silently, he'd slip into the garden, through the conservatory – and into her waiting arms and welcoming bed.

'Are you going to tell me what's happened?' Laura faced her across their kitchen table on the Wednesday afternoon. 'I haven't seen you look so radiant since you got engaged to my brother … An hour ago I even heard you singing.'

Beatrice said, 'I have so much to sing about.'

'It's Alex, isn't it?' Laura poured their tea.

'Of course it's Alex. And before you ask, yes, we're lovers.'

Laura's mouth dropped. *'What?'*

'Why are you so surprised? We've known each other for two months, since the beginning of May. He's the most extraordinary person I've ever met.'

'And may I ask *where* you've – '

'His bed,' Beatrice said blithely. 'And my bed … And yesterday we found a tree in the middle of a wood near … God, I've no idea where we were.' She blushed. 'But I can remember exactly what we did.'

Laura put down her cup. 'My darling Beatrice, have you gone completely mad?'

'Of course not. This is the sanest, most perfect thing I've ever done in my life.'

'You do realise you're putting *everything* in jeopardy … Your home, your marriage … Victor will be sure to find out. He won't stand for it.'

Beatrice explained how she'd found the revolting perfumed handkerchief.

'So?' Laura asked, her face pale, her eyes dark with anxiety. 'It doesn't prove anything. Victor could have picked it up in the street, for all you know … Besides, men are allowed to take the odd mistress from time to time.'

'And their wives aren't allowed to have lovers? Is that what you're saying? Because if you are, it's too late.'

'It's *not* too late, Bea. You must end the affair today, tomorrow, right now, before it goes any further … There's absolutely no future in your relationship. Alex will go back to his job in New York, and you'll be left here to pick up the pieces. If, that is, you have any pieces left!'

Beatrice bit her lip. 'But I don't want it to end. I can't live without him, Laura. I simply can't.'

'Don't give me that insufferable twaddle.' Laura joined her at the stove, flinging an arm around her shoulders. 'You've built an entire life without Alexander Hertzler. You've got me, the business, a wealthy husband, houses, gardens, nephews and two beautiful nieces. Don't you *dare* throw us all away for a crazy night of passion under the stars.'

Beatrice turned to face her oldest and dearest friend.

'Is that all it's been, Laura? You make it sound so trite and ridiculous.' Tears stung. 'He's the most wonderful lover. Tender, passionate, considerate. Driving with him in Hermione has been bliss. On Monday, I drove us both back to Charlbury from Wolvercote. I could do it so easily. It was the furthest I've ever driven. And all because of him. You couldn't possibly understand.'

'My darling Bea, I understand only too well. If Victor gets to hear about your affair, when the gossip spreads, it'll reach our clients too, you can be sure of that. It could ruin us in a couple of weeks … Please, Beatrice, if you love me, if I mean *anything* to you, listen to me and take my advice. End it now, before it's too late to do anything.'

Beatrice spent the rest of Wednesday and the whole of Thursday in an agony of indecision. Her wild joy faded into sanity. She knew Laura was right. Being in London, away from Alex, helped the reckless frenzy of love to cool. At night she dreamed about him, his name on her lips and in her mind from the moment she woke. But he wasn't beside her and she couldn't hear his voice.

On Friday she sat down with Laura, tears pouring down her cheeks.

'I'll have to take the coward's way out. If I meet Alex again on Monday, we'll be in each other's arms the moment we're free to do so.'

She wrote him a short note. She loved him as she'd never loved anyone before, and probably never would again. But their meetings had to end. She was sure he'd understand. Before she could change her mind, she left Elm Row for the post office, and ran down the hill. She slid the wretched envelope into its dark landing place.

Three weeks later, in St John's Wood, she woke feeling nauseous. The fish pie she'd eaten with her husband the night before must be the culprit. She didn't feel like breakfast, told Victor she had a headache but it would soon pass, and left in a cab for Hampstead on an empty stomach.

London throbbed with heat. The air was already thick with dust. The stink of dung rose in clouds, making her feel worse. She shook her head at the coffee Laura offered, and ran into the kitchen to drink a glass of water.

At midday, as every room in the house sat heavy with trapped beams of sun, the telephone rang in her study. She took the call and made a note in her diary. *Wednesday 2 August: 3.00 pm: Lady Merton and her daughter: Wedding dress and full trousseau.* She watched as the words she'd written jumped up and down in front of her eyes.

Then the world around her turned a relentless inky black, shot through with tiny sparkling stars … Her legs gave way beneath her.

Laura picked her up off the floor, made her sit down properly, brought a cool wet flannel for her forehead and a cup of strong, sweet tea.

'Thank you, darling.' She drank the entire cup and put it down. 'I've no idea what happened … One minute I was on the telephone … The next – ' She picked up the flannel and pressed it against her eyes.

She said slowly, 'My period is ten days late.'

Laura knelt beside her. 'Well, blow me down with a feather.'

'I'm pregnant, aren't I?' She held out her arms. 'Oh, God, darling … I'm having a baby. I never thought it would happen again. But this is exactly how I felt when I was pregnant with Ralph's child.'

'And now you are having Alex's.' Laura held her close. 'Only *this* time, we'll make it happen, won't we? All nine months of it.'

Beatrice put Laura's hands on her stomach. 'This time, I promise we will.' She stood up, as the room rocked on its axis. 'Of course, I'll have to *tell* him, won't I?'

'Why?' Laura looked up at her. 'Why does Alex ever have to know?'

'Because he lost *his* daughter.' Beatrice held on to the arm of the nearest chair to steady her small universe. 'Her name was Sylvia. And I might just be able to give him another little girl.'

'But you said you'd finish things with him.' Laura

stood up, her face flushed with rage. 'You *promised* me you'd end it.'

'I *did* end it. I've been rattling around Chandos without him for three of the longest weeks of my life. I've watched him coming back through the garden after riding Victor's horses in the early morning and I never once went out to greet him. I've spotted him driving through the village in Hermione and I never even waved acknowledgement. I've walked past Theo's cottage without knocking on the door. It's been ghastly, Laura, a loneliness I can't begin to describe, but I've managed it.

'But I have to tell him, soon, that I'm carrying his child. There's a limit to how cruel I can be. He has a right to know.'

'And what will you do about Victor?'

Beatrice felt the blood leave every limb of her body. 'Take him to bed with me as soon as I can … I'll have to pretend the child is his. I don't have any choice.'

On Saturday morning, she scribbled Alex a short note. *Meet me as usual in Hermione on Monday for cakes and lemonade. B.* She left Chandos and walked through to Church Street. Theo was riding with Victor. Hermione wasn't parked outside the cottage. She pushed the note through the door and moved quickly down the road.

She spent the rest of the weekend preparing to seduce her husband. They had guests from Oxford on the Saturday night who arrived late and did not leave until midnight. It would have to be Sunday evening. She'd ask Cook to prepare roast lamb, Victor's favourite. Make sure he drank a lot of red wine but not too much.

She wanted him to remember.

She'd wear a low-cut dress.

At the end of the meal she'd invite Victor to her bed. And make sure he remained there until morning.

Of course, she'd been through this same ritual many times before. Often with a sense of obligation. The time of the month was right. It was her duty to make love to him. But never before had she gone through the familiar pattern of the evening with such a sense of dread.

As she dressed for dinner, a wave of guilt took her by the throat and threatened to engulf her. As if she were planning to be unfaithful to Alex.

'I knew you couldn't keep away from me.' Relief rang in his beautiful American voice. Triumph sparkled in his eyes. He glanced at Beatrice as he drove to Leafield and the cool shade of its church. 'I couldn't believe my eyes when I read your letter … I knew you didn't really mean it.'

'Oh, but I did,' she said. Alex looked thinner. She knew the past few weeks had been as hard for him as they had been for her. 'I love you with all my heart, with every scrap of my soul. But I can't see you again.'

'Then what are we doing now?' He grated the gears. 'Why are you putting us both through this torment? If I can't touch you, make love to you, what's this all about?'

'It's about us being together one last time.' She stared out of the window at the harvested fields, the swoop of crows skimming them for food. Her mouth felt dry, her tongue reluctant to form the words she needed to say.

'I've something to tell you, face to face, that I couldn't possibly send in a letter.'

Alex parked Hermione and they climbed out of the car. They walked past the church and sat against the wall that overlooked the graveyard. He took her hand.

'Tell me now, my darling Beatrice, tell me quickly in

195

words that make the utmost sense before I faint from heat and die of love.'

'You won't believe your ears but I wanted you to know, almost as soon as I did … I'm having your child.'

Alex dropped her hand and scrambled to his feet. 'But you told me that could never happen. You said you were – '

'Barren.' The word fell like a stone on the burned grass. 'I assumed I was. Victor and I have been married for four years … Last May, I even consulted Theo. He told me I was fit and healthy, there was hope for me yet … But I'd given up hoping and praying.'

'And now?' Alex said wildly. 'It's such marvellous news … Are you sure?'

'Quite sure.' Beatrice looked up at him as he stood staring down at her against the midday sun. 'Remember I told you about Ralph Brightman, being engaged to him when I was still a student? I was three weeks pregnant when he was killed. The following week, I lost the baby. Laura was the only person who knew … And Laura is the only person who must ever know that the baby I'm carrying is yours.'

Alex dropped to his knees. 'You mean, you're staying with Victor? You're choosing to go on being his wife?'

'I don't *have* a choice.' A wave of nausea climbed from her stomach to her throat. 'Please, Alex, you've got to understand. Nobody else must ever know. Especially not Theo, whom I admire so much. Especially never him.'

She planned to give Victor the good news over Sunday lunch in two weeks' time.

The days of early August continued to be intolerably hot, but when she woke that Sunday morning, although the air felt heavy and humid, the sky had lost its radiant Italian blue and was already overcast.

Victor returned from his ride alone: Theo had gone to Scotland on a fortnight's holiday. He went to wash and change. She waited for him in the dining room, her palms damp with sweat, her cotton bodice clinging to her ribs, her heart beating so fast she'd never be able to swallow anything.

She watched Victor walk into the room, sit at the table and flap open his serviette. Outside the window she noticed the sky had darkened. She heard the faintest rumble of thunder growl upwards from the river.

'There's going to be one hell of a storm,' he said.

She pushed the cold chicken and salad around her plate, pretending to eat. She stared at the two small bowls of strawberries and cream, admiring the contrast of colours. A second, more ominous snarl of thunder echoed through the room. She repeated in her head the words she'd so carefully rehearsed all weekend. She waited until there wasn't a servant in sight and the dining-room door had firmly closed.

And then she heard the sound of her own voice, together with one she barely recognised: the splatter of water on the glass roof of the conservatory.

Finally it had begun to rain.

'I'm so glad we can spend the rest of the day together, Victor.'

'Oh?' He swallowed a heaped teaspoon of berries and cream. 'And why is that, then, dear?'

'Because,' Beatrice said, her words so dutifully polished, supposedly so wonderful to hear, 'I'm delighted to say I can finally give you the news you've waited for, over the last four years.'

Victor's spoon hovered in mid-air. 'Which is?'

'I'm going to have your child.'

The spoon and its contents clattered to the floor.

'Forgive me.' Victor's face turned ashen. '*What* did you just say?'

A third clap of thunder shook against the roof.

She said more loudly, to beat the noise, to repeat her message until her husband understood, 'I'm pregnant, Victor. Isn't it wonderful? I'm going to have your child.'

Victor stared at her, his eyes black, his fists clenched, his mouth clamped in a thin straight line. He said so quietly it was almost a whisper, 'Much though I'd like to congratulate you, Beatrice, I'm sorry to say that's quite impossible.'

'Of course it's not impossible! It's what we've both been longing for. And I'm absolutely sure about it … I've missed my last period … I've felt a bit nauseous in the mornings, but that's only normal, isn't it?' She rattled on. She needed to make her story sound entirely believable, absolutely waterproof. Every detail needed to be accurate, so there could be no questions asked.

'It must have happened when we had that wonderful night together several weeks ago … You remember, don't you?'

Victor threw his serviette on to the table, flung his chair aside and stood up. Through gritted teeth he said, 'You don't understand, you stupid woman. I'm sterile as a suet pudding. Shall I spell it out in words of one syllable? *I can only fire blanks.*'

For a long ghastly moment, Beatrice was sure she was going to faint.

'That can't be true.'

'I'll tell you one last time. I'm completely and utterly unable to father your child or, for that matter, anyone else's!'

She clung to the arms of her chair. 'How long have you known?'

'That I'm not the real knife in the box?' Victor turned

198

towards the window. Raindrops had begun to fall against the pane in long curling lines, like giant snakes. He held trembling fingers against them. 'For absolute certainty, since January.'

He choked a sob. She'd never ever seen him shed a single tear.

'I went to see a doctor in the New Year.' He wheeled round to face her. 'I was thirty-seven before I married you. I used to visit prostitutes in London. I'm not proud of it, but that was the life I led. One of them, when I was only twenty, gave me a foul disease. I was warned it might have fatal long-term consequences but I refused to believe it.'

A wave of anger shook her. 'And you never thought to tell me the truth … All this time you've made me believe the fault was mine. You're a monster.'

'Yes, well.' Victor had the grace to blush. 'It's what men do, isn't it?' His eyes blazed with fury. 'And as for you … I've listened to the gossip. I've seen you together. He's eaten at my table, he's ridden my horses and now he's taken my wife … You don't need to tell me who the father is. It's Alexander bloody Hertzler, isn't it? Teaching you to drive, indeed. I *knew* something was going on, in broad daylight, under my own roof.'

Victor mopped his face with a handkerchief. The scent of hyacinths rose into the air. 'You're not my wife. You're nothing but a despicable little whore.'

Beatrice looked up at him. A flash of lightning scorched across the sky. It seemed to burn her eyes out of her head.

She blinked in the startling whiteness of the light.

When she looked across the room, Victor had disappeared.

She ran into the conservatory, shouting his name.

Five minutes later, she saw him galloping away through the garden and down to the river beyond.

Alexander

Alex stood in Theo's garden in the pouring rain.

He lifted his face to the sky and felt the drops pouring over his hair, on to his hands, through his cotton shirt and down his back. The green scent of the wet grass filled his lungs. The relief, after all those weeks of sweltering heat, made him want to sob with gratitude. He longed to strip off his clothes and dance around the garden, stark naked, singing for joy.

Nobody would see him. Theo had gone to Scotland on holiday. He'd asked Alex to go with him.

'We can drive through the Lake District on our way to Edinburgh. It'll be magical. I must get away from my ailing women for a couple of weeks.'

But Alex had said no thank you. He didn't tell his brother he was waiting for something to happen in Charlbury, waiting with all the patience he could muster for the beautiful Beatrice to send him an invitation, to come once again to his door.

His clothes soaking, rain streaming through his hair, he sloshed indoors to dry his body and change into fresh clothes. He'd wait until the rain stopped before he went out again.

Wearing a pair of cream linen trousers and a loose cotton shirt, he padded out of his bedroom. He'd opened all the windows that morning to get some air. Now he stepped across the landing to Theo's bedroom. Rain poured through the open window on to the floor. He moved quickly to close it.

At which point he saw Beatrice crossing the road towards him, walking fast, trying to keep her umbrella from blowing inside out, her long dress soaking at the hem.

He flew down the stairs and opened the door.

She fell into his arms.

'Thank God you're here.' She leaned against him. He could feel the heat of her limbs, the pounding of her heart. 'It's Victor. We had the most terrible row. He knows you're the father. He can't ... ' She hesitated, gasping for breath. 'He doesn't know what he's doing. He went out on a horse more than an hour ago in a desperate rage ... Please, Alex, you'll know where he'll be. Could you go and look for him? Bring him back to Chandos?'

'Of course.'

He thrust his bare feet into his shoes, flung on his raincoat, stuffed his keys into his pocket. He held Beatrice for a precious moment in his arms.

'I'll race to the stables and ride one of the strong geldings. Don't worry, I'll find Victor, I promise. I'll see you back at Chandos.'

He left her standing there and slammed the door.

The torrential rain had already created puddles along his path. The stones in the churchyard felt slippery and dangerous. He ran as fast as he could, but he took it carefully.

If he slipped and fell, his search for the man he most loathed in all the world would be over before it had begun.

In the stables the three geldings stood quietly as always: well-groomed, well-fed and well-behaved, in spite of the rain hammering on the roof and the continuing bellows of thunder. Victor had taken Domino. Alex cursed under his breath. The mare was the weakest of the horses, especially in a storm. Why had Victor risked his favourite steed in such appalling conditions?

He threw a saddle over Diamond and led the gelding to the stable door. The horse shied briefly at the vicious weather, but he murmured words of comfort as he mounted, gazing over the garden.

Victor would have crossed the river and the railway line by the bridge, and then made his way across the fields towards Cornbury Park. Alex knew the way so well he could have ridden blindfold.

The rain was falling so heavily he might almost have had a real blindfold over his eyes. The heavens had opened with a vengeance, spewing up after those months of summer drought on every inch of dry land. He took Diamond at a trot, unwilling to force the horse's natural speed into a gallop. Holding the reins in one hand, wiping the rain out of his eyes with the other, he began to shout Victor's name.

After an hour, his throat felt sore, his back ached. Diamond had begun to slow down, his mane dripping with water. His leather saddle felt like pulp. For the second time that day, he was soaked to the skin. He must be carrying his own weight in water – and Diamond would be feeling it.

He turned back from the park and started for home.

It was not until he'd almost reached the river that he saw Domino. The mare was lying in a crumpled heap on the river bed. The torrents of water washed over her.

He dug his heels in. Urging the gelding on, he forced Diamond into a final gallop. The brilliant horse gave him everything he had. As they drew close to the river, he saw Victor lying the other side of the mare, his body sunk in the river, his head flung back on to the side of the bank.

Alex drew up as close as he could to the fallen mare and her rider. He peeled himself off Diamond, muttered directions for the gelding to wait, and slithered towards the bodies.

'Victor? Can you hear me? What the hell have you done to yourself?'

He knelt beside the man, laying his fingers on the pulse in Victor's neck.

'If you can hear me, give me a sign. Anything. Lift your hand. Open your eyes. Talk to me.'

Victor lay completely motionless. Alex stood up. He'd go to get help as fast as he could.

He'd squelched a few steps towards Diamond when he heard Victor mutter something. He stumbled back on his tracks, a streak of lightning for a moment blinding him.

'Help me.' Victor's voice came so quietly he had to bend double to hear him. Victor reached out his hand. *'If you get me out of here, you can have my wife.'*

His eyes opened and closed again on a face as white as chalk.

Alex threw back his head and almost spat at Victor. He clenched his fists.

How dare the man imply that Beatrice was up for barter? Had he got a heart and soul? He felt like flinging himself on Diamond and galloping away. He'd tell Beatrice he was sorry, he'd searched everywhere, her husband had vanished in the storm. Somebody else would find the stinking bastard and his beautiful mare when the rain had eased. They would *both* be dead – and it wouldn't be his fault.

But then he heard the voice of his beloved father ringing in his ears, as if his Pa were standing beside him, holding his wet hands, stroking his hair.

'Our job is to serve, Al, come what may. No matter who calls us or what they need. Our only job is to get them well again.'

He scrambled through the mud to Diamond, drawing the horse as close as he could towards Victor. He took a deep breath, filling his lungs with the scents of the river bed, trying to find the strength he needed. He managed to lift Victor on to Diamond. Carefully, painfully, step by step, he led the horse and its heavy, wet, bleeding burden back to the gardens ahead of them.

Beatrice stood inside the conservatory, but she came running out to them in the rain.

Alex called out, 'I'd almost given up. I rode everywhere I could think of, shouting Victor's name, yelling my lungs out. It wasn't until I'd turned on my tracks to come home that I found him.'

He pushed wet hair out of his eyes.

'Tell your groom that Domino is dead. The mare's lying in the river.' He looked more closely at Victor. 'Your husband's unconscious, Beatrice. I don't know how much damage has been done. Get him to the Radcliffe as quickly as you can.'

'Victor's chauffeur is waiting in the Daimler. Can you carry Victor indoors for me? We can put some dry clothes on him and get him in the car.'

'Yes, just about. I've done my best, darling. The rest is up to you.'

Beatrice took his hands in hers. 'I shall love you for doing this until my dying day.'

He staggered away from Chandos, every limb aching, soaked to the skin – and sick to his stomach as Victor's words rang in his head. He felt in his pocket for his keys and opened the door to Theo's cottage.

On the doormat, he peeled off his clothes, leaving them in a stinking muddy puddle on the floor. Pulling on the banisters, he hauled himself upstairs. Shivering with cold and deadly fatigue, he flung on his dressing gown.

He threw himself on his bed and was in an instant asleep.

Charlotte

Charlotte stared crossly at her aunt over the tea table in the Chandos garden. She seemed to be behaving rather oddly. She and Alex kept laughing at private jokes, finishing each other's sentences. When Auntie Bea's serviette floated by mistake on to the grass, Alex leaped to pick it up, handing it back to her. 'I believe this belongs to you, my lady,' he said. They laughed together into each other's eyes all over again.

Even when she'd played tennis with Alex, he'd kept glancing towards the terrace, as if he were looking for someone, rather than concentrating on her and the tennis ball. She hoped she looked particularly fetching in the new long skirt and figure-hugging blouse that Auntie Bea had made.

Didn't he realise this might be the last tennis match they'd ever play together, just the two of them? The last tea they'd ever drink at Chandos? Tomorrow she was being hauled off to London with Foxie. The marvellous summer with the more than marvellous Alex was coming to its devastating end.

Over tea, he was so busy chatting to Auntie Bea she could hardly get a word in edgeways. It wasn't until he'd got up to leave and walked round the side path to the front drive that she made herself race after him.

'I wanted to give you this.' She dug in her pocket for the small box she'd put carefully away in her cupboard before Easter. She'd bought it for Sebastian, but that felt like a hundred years ago. Anyway, he'd been nothing but a silly young boy with an unspeakable mother. She had much better plans for it now. 'It's to say thank you for everything … I hope you like it.'

Alex looked embarrassed.

'A tie-pin,' he said. 'Thank you very much. It's really elegant. I'll enjoy wearing it.' He backed away, giving her a mock salute. 'Goodbye and very good luck with everything.'

Any hope that he might kiss her goodbye when nobody else was looking, or better still suggest they meet in London because he couldn't bear to be without her, faded abruptly into the heat and dust of the summer afternoon. She watched him walk away, and tried hard not to cry.

Miriam dangled her little finger in Violet's milk-dribbling mouth.

'Who's the most beautiful baby in the world?' she cooed. Emile stood with his arm around her, nuzzling her neck.

'Now, just look who's travelled all the way from Oxfordshire to see you! Your older sister, Charlotte! Say hello to little Violet, darling. Isn't she the loveliest baby you ever did see?'

Reluctantly, Charlotte took a closer look. Violet had a mop of sweaty dark hair, bright pink lips and a nose full of snot. She smelled of sick.

She moved away. 'I'm going upstairs to unpack.'

'I've advertised for a nanny.' Miriam planted a long kiss on Emile's cheek. 'I've got a couple of applicants coming for interviews this afternoon … But I wondered whether you'd like to look after Violet for us this evening. Emile and I have tickets for the opera … It's been *ages* since we did anything glamorous together in London. And now we're married, I want to show off my new husband … You won't mind, will you, darling? Violet will be absolutely no trouble, I promise.'

'This has got to stop!' She'd marched upstairs to find Foxie who was packing the twins' trunk in their bedroom. Emile had taken them to the park.

'What has, dear?' Foxie reached to a top shelf for the buckets and spades.

'Being carted off like a parcel, without being asked what I want to do.'

'Going down to St Ives again is hardly being carted off!' Foxie dabbed her top lip with her sleeve. 'London is so hot at the moment. Cornwall's sea breezes will be just what the doctor ordered, and wonderful for the baby. You'll be able to walk on the beach again – '

'We've been back in Kensington for *two days*! I want to see Rosalind, go to parties with my friends … I won't be able to do anything I really want.'

'Look, Charlotte.' Foxie crumpled on to a low chair by the twins' bedside. 'You really must stop complaining. Your mother's doing her best to give you a lovely summer holiday by the sea. Next spring she's promised you'll be presented at Court. You'll have plenty of time for your friends, dozens of parties to go to, and lots of nice young suitors asking for your hand in marriage … Until then, you'll just have to be patient.'

'If Mother thinks I'm going to spend months sitting around, twiddling my thumbs and looking after my silly baby sister, she'd better think again.'

'But Violet is *adorable*.' Foxie folded an armful of trousers into the trunk. 'Anyway, we now have a very smart new nanny to do the donkey work.'

'Just as well.' Charlotte glanced at her reflection in a wall mirror. She smoothed her hair and straightened her collar. 'I *detest* babies. I shall only marry a man who doesn't want children.'

Foxie sighed. 'Could we cross that bridge when we come to it?'

For the next six weeks, she fell dutifully into line and played happy families at the seaside. She ate meals in the dining room at Tregenna and spoke French to keep Foxie happy. Every morning she walked in the gardens or ran down the steep hill to the beach. She shopped for trinkets in St Ives, helped the twins fly their kite, smiled approval at their nanny, tried not to look too closely at the way Emile kissed her mother, avoided Miriam herself whenever possible and cooed ridiculous babyish nonsense words at Violet at every appropriate moment.

But all the while she was hatching a secret plan. It had nothing to do with any of her family, but everything to do with Alex. He was the only person she could think about. Her thoughts and dreams and passionate desires revolved entirely around him.

He'd spent so much time with her at Chandos. He'd rescued her so splendidly when she'd been ill. He'd told her about some of the operations he'd performed in New York, described the other staff at St Luke's, talked about his best friend Leonard – even about his own daughter who'd died so tragically of typhoid fever.

What glorious long afternoons they'd spent together! Walking in Chandos's gardens, playing tennis, having tea on the lawn. She remembered the Coronation celebrations in Charlbury, how they'd been to them together, just like a proper couple. One of the women in the crowd had fainted in the heat. Alex had revived her, made sure she'd recovered, that she had someone to take her safely home.

It was that tiny incident that first gave her an idea. The more she thought about it, the better it seemed. It started to grow from an innocent seedling into a full-blown military plan. She just needed to decide when she could put it into decisive, organised action. She assumed Alex was still in Charlbury, but she knew that if she hesitated much longer, he might return to New York. Her plan was ambitious enough without her having to go *that* far to see him!

Then something happened one Saturday morning in the middle of August that spurred her on. She'd been waiting in Miriam's bedroom so they could go down to breakfast together. Miriam had given their nanny two days off to visit friends in Penzance. She dumped a clean, beautifully dressed Violet into Charlotte's arms.

'Could you carry her to the dining room, darling? I need to do my hair. Emile and I will be with you in ten minutes. Foxie and the twins have already gone down.'

Charlotte tightened her arms carefully around the baby. She left Miriam's room and walked downstairs. In the foyer, a group of new guests stood by the reception desk, signing papers and collecting keys. They moved towards Charlotte as she moved inexorably towards them. A couple and their three tall children: a boy and two girls. One of them had ash-blond hair and blue eyes that shone like sapphires.

'Good *heavens*,' Lady Manners said loudly. 'That Stallworthy family must be staying here again, or should I call them Dubois?' As an aside, but loud enough for Charlotte to hear, she added, 'I hope to God that's not *your* baby, Sebastian!'

'Don't be ridiculous, Mother.' Sebastian bowed briefly to Charlotte as they passed. 'Good morning, Miss Stallworthy. Another beautiful day?'

She did not return his greeting. She marched into the dining room, sat next to Foxie, bouncing Violet up and down on her knees, her face flame red, her heart burning with anger.

She spent the rest of Saturday and all Sunday trying to avoid the Manners' family.

It proved impossible. They sat talking in unexpected corners of the hotel; lingered on every staircase; ate all their meals in the dining room. On Sunday afternoon, she spotted Sebastian in the garden, walking deliberately towards her. She raced away, scampering down the hill into St Ives until she was sure he'd given up his quest and gone away. Somewhere, anywhere. Just leave me alone.

She woke at dawn on Monday morning. She'd already laid out her best travelling suit, her hat, her gloves, her bag with enough travelling money, her smartest walking shoes, shaken free of sand and polished until they shone.

She left a note addressed to Miriam propped on her pillow.

Half an hour later, she walked out of Tregenna into its dew-drenched gardens. The sky, filled with a swoop of seagulls, beckoned its greeting. The air smelled of the sea.

At the bottom of the hill she turned into the road leading to the station.

Smart, clean, organised and very pleased with herself, she waited impatiently for the early morning train to Paddington.

Alexander

He woke on that same Monday morning feeling stiff, bruised and starving. A hot bath and an enormous breakfast helped. He hoped Diamond had survived her ordeal. He wondered how the groom would retrieve Domino's body. It couldn't possibly be done without the help of at least one other strong man.

But there was no way he could face the stables or any of the geldings, or offer any help whatsoever. He kept remembering Beatrice's pale face, her wet dress, the desperation and then the gratitude in those violet-blue eyes. He longed to know how she was – indeed, how Victor was – but he didn't dare walk to Chandos to find out.

He tried valiantly to reassure himself. Beatrice would let him know if there was any firm news, either good or bad. She had Victor's chauffeur and the Daimler to get her to and from the hospital.

He took Hermione for a spin, hardly knowing or caring where he went. Some of the narrow lanes still shone with rain. He wandered into the village, past The Bell, stifling an urge to go into the pub, drink a bottle of whisky and several pints of beer. Instead he went to the baker's. He bought a loaf of fresh white bread, ate half of it for lunch, smeared with butter and chunks of cheddar cheese. The lemonade he drank instead of beer reminded him of picnics with Beatrice.

When he couldn't bear to wait a moment longer, he made his way to Chandos. The Daimler wasn't in the drive. The housekeeper answered the door. Mrs Davenport had returned to bath and change, but she'd gone back to the Radcliffe. Mr Davenport's condition was very serious. He'd been placed in intensive care.

'Please,' he said, his heart in his mouth, 'give Mrs Davenport my best wishes. If there's anything I can do to help, anything at all, she's to let me know.'

Disconsolate and helpless, he limped back to Theo's cottage. As he opened the door he realised with an almighty shock that he was longing for Victor to die.

The afternoon stretched interminably into early evening. He picked up the soaking clothes he'd left on the doormat, washed them in Lux soap flakes and hung them out to dry. He pottered around Theo's garden, sweeping up damp leaves, pruning the roses, cutting back fallen branches that had snapped beneath the onslaught of the storm. He read the same page of a medical journal fifteen times, and gave up. He drank some tea and then a bowl of tomato soup. He kept glancing out of the front window, willing Beatrice miraculously to appear.

When the doorbell rang he flung himself out of his chair. At last! It could only be her. He didn't know whether he should be praying for good news, bad news or no news. She'd come to see him, she was carrying his child. Those two miraculous occurrences were all that mattered.

He ran a hand through his hair and flew to answer the door.

'Hello, Alex,' Charlotte said. 'I hope I'm not disturbing you … May I come in?'

'Good heavens.' Flabbergasted, he stood in the doorway. 'I thought you'd gone back to Kensington … Have you come from Chandos?'

'No, I've just travelled up from St Ives.' Charlotte's dress and gloves were spattered in fine dust. Dark shadows lurked beneath her eyes. 'My family are on holiday in Cornwall … I couldn't bear it a minute longer. I simply had to see you.' She looked longingly over his shoulder into the hall. 'May I come in? I haven't eaten all day and I'm dying of thirst.'

'I'm so sorry. Of course.' He stood aside and closed the door behind her. 'Come into the kitchen. I'm waiting to hear from your aunt. Victor was in a terrible accident yesterday. He's in hospital.'

'I'm sorry to hear that.'

Hardly listening, Charlotte sat down abruptly on the nearest chair. She took off her hat, wiped her forehead with a dusty glove. She looked close to tears, which had nothing to do with Victor.

'I've run away from them all at Tregenna … Nobody knows where I am.'

'*What?* You mean your mother – '

'Good God, no. Miriam doesn't give a jot about me. New husband, new baby, new life. I just get in the way, unless she needs me to babysit.'

'I'm sure that can't be true.' He thought, I must get rid of this pathetic child as quickly as I can, before Beatrice arrives to talk to me and finds her here. 'Let's take your tea through to the garden room. The moment you've drunk it, I'll go with you to find your aunt.'

'No.' Charlotte's eyes followed him around the room. 'It's *you* I've come to see, not any of my family. You see, I've had the most wonderful idea. I've been thinking about it for weeks. When we said goodbye last month, it almost broke my heart.'

Slowly and carefully, he poured the tea. He handed Charlotte a cup. 'I hope you don't mean – '

'I'm *madly* in love with you.' Charlotte looked up at him, her cup rattling, her eyes misty with tears. 'I know you *like* me. Why else would you have spent so much time with me all summer?'

'My dear Charlotte – '

'No, let me finish. Please, just let me get the words out before I fall off my chair.' Charlotte's hat slid to the floor. She dropped her gloves trying to pick it up. Her cup of tea slipped from her hands in sympathy.

'I want to marry you, and live here with you in Charlbury. You could take over as the village doctor. The one who's already here, he's at least a hundred years old and planning to retire. I heard the maids talking about it.

'You could take over, and I'll work as your receptionist. I could learn about nursing and medicine and all that stuff. I'll be so helpful, at your side through thick and thin.' She bent to pick up the empty cup, staring at the stain on the pale rug.

'Heavens, what an awful mess. Could you pour me some more? I'm so terribly thirsty. Thank you. Well, my dearest darling Alex. Please say yes. I wouldn't want a huge wedding or anything and Auntie Bea will make me the most wonderful frock … She'll be delighted to hear our news. What do you say?'

He wondered whether she was suffering from heatstroke or had for a short and terrible time gone completely mad.

'Dearest Charlotte, I'm really flattered. You've come all this way, and you've paid me the most enormous compliment.'

He paused, not wanting to say it, to tell her, to spell it out. He had no choice. His back was flat as a pancake against the wall. If he told Charlotte, she'd tell Beatrice.

So be it. There was no other way.

'The thing is,' he said, 'I've got to turn down your marvellous offer. I need to go back to New York.' He held up a hand to silence her protest. 'And it will have to be without you. You are young and pretty, and I'm sure you'll find your ideal husband … But it can't be me.

'You see, Charlotte, I'm a married man. My little daughter died of typhoid fever but I managed to rescue my wife.' He picked up one of Lillian's postcards he'd received a fortnight ago. 'See? This is from her. She's been touring Europe with her parents to get over the grief of losing our child. We haven't seen each other for many months. But I'm not free to marry anybody else, not even you.'

He helped the sobbing girl across the road, through the graveyard and made sure she set off down the Chandos drive. He spotted the empty Daimler sitting there. So Beatrice had returned without coming to see him.

He spun on his heels and went back to Theo's cottage, where he counted the hours and spent an entirely sleepless night.

He rose at dawn, his throat sore, his head throbbing, his heart thundering with dread. He bathed and dressed, made coffee, swallowed it and raced out of the cottage as if it were on fire. He'd stand at the gates of Chandos until Beatrice emerged.

As the church clock struck nine, he spotted her at the

216

door, looking pale, but polished and elegant, the chauffeur beside her. He begged to talk to her for five minutes, in private. She nodded. The chauffeur went to sit in the car.

He asked after Victor. Beatrice said he was still unconscious. The doctors had given her very little encouragement that anything would change for the better. But there was always hope.

She held herself straight as a ramrod, deliberately leaving several feet between them, as if they were strangers.

He asked after Charlotte. Beatrice said the girl was still asleep. She'd rung Miriam at Tregenna. A car would be sent to collect Charlotte and drive her to Kensington. Foxie would join her there in case she threatened to run away again. Beatrice said bitterly she had quite enough to worry about, now that Victor was so ill.

Then he managed to blurt out the words he had to say.

'I'm so terribly sorry I never told you about Lillian. I hope you will forgive me. That night we first met, I'd have spelled it out, but we were interrupted by Foxie. Do you remember? It was on the tip of my tongue, but – '

'It doesn't matter now. Charlotte made quite sure I got the ghastly message, loud and clear.'

He bent his head. He said, 'I love you more than words can ever say.'

He took her hand and raised it to his lips. Hers were white with pain. He watched her turn her back on him. The Daimler sped away in a cloud of dust.

As it settled in its wake, he knew he'd reached the very end of the line.

He climbed the stairs at Theo's and packed his suitcase. He hauled it downstairs and sat at the desk in the garden room, writing Beatrice a letter. He climbed into Hermione and drove the car into the Chandos drive. He left the letter on the dashboard, climbed out of the car and walked back to Theo's.

An hour later he stood on the platform at Charlbury station, waiting for the train to Paddington.

'Good morning, dearest bro!'

Theo stood up to give him a long hug, and then sat down again at the breakfast table in Regent's Park. 'I got in late last night. You were spark out.' He ate a mouthful of boiled egg, looking bronzed and shining and relaxed. 'It's so great to *see* you here ... How have you been?'

'Fine, thank you.' Alex poured a cup of coffee. Well, if he were going to tell Theo a pack of lies, he might as well lay it on with a trowel. 'I've never been better.'

'I had *such* a wonderful vacation,' Theo rattled on, oblivious. 'The dales in Yorkshire are glorious, and Edinburgh is a tremendous city. Lots of heavy granite buildings and fantastic views.' He looked across the table at his brother. 'It was marvellous to have all the time in the world, for a change, just to do whatever I wanted, all day long ... Of course, you must know what *that* feels like, after your months of freedom!'

'Yes,' he said. 'I do ... I've had an extraordinary sabbatical. I haven't swallowed a drop of liquor since the day you walked through my New York door, and I feel ten years younger. It's been ... ' he searched for the words, 'a brilliant English summer. Perfect in every way.' That was the trouble with lying. Once you started, you couldn't stop. 'I can't thank you enough.'

'I'm real glad to hear it – '

'But now,' he took a deep breath, 'I've decided it's time to go back to my own crazily busy world. Back to St Luke's before I'm too old to chop guys open and make them feel a whole lot better.'

Theo held his serviette to his mouth. 'Oh?' His lips emerged, pristine and surprised. 'Why's that, then? We're still in the lovely month of August. I thought you were going to hang around London for a bit, see the sights, go to the theatre. Spin out the golden days a while longer.'

'So did I.' Golden days never last, buddy. They can be over just like that. Flick the switch and you're back at square one. 'Thing is, my great pal Len Grant – you know, the guy who wrote to you – he's getting hitched. He wants me to be his best man. I can't possibly refuse, not after all he did for me when I was down among the dead men.' And just take a look at me now.

Theo stood up to clap him on the shoulder. 'I shall miss you like hell, dearest bro. Charlbury won't be the same without you.'

Beatrice

As their chauffeur drove her back to Chandos from the Radcliffe Infirmary, Beatrice sat against the leather seat and closed her eyes, much too exhausted to sleep. Her mind buzzed with so many concerns she felt she'd drown in a cesspit of worries.

Having a hysterical Charlotte on her hands yesterday had become the least of them. Being told by her dusty, tear-stained niece that the man she, Beatrice, had adored throughout the summer had been committing adultery with her turned her small world upside-down all over again.

Victor had confessed to sterility. Alex had a living, breathing spouse.

Was there *anyone* in her life she could trust?

The moment the Daimler drove into the Chandos drive, Beatrice spied Hermione parked in a discreet corner, slightly away from the house. Her heart leaped with hope and desire. Was Alex sitting in it, waiting for her, in order to tell her he intended to divorce Lillian, that he wanted her to leave Victor and marry him?

She must be mad even to think those crazy things – even to hope. Anyway, Hermione was empty. Peering through the car window, she spotted a letter addressed to her lying on the dashboard. She stuffed it in her bag. She longed to climb into Hermione and drive. Anywhere. Just to get away.

Upstairs in her bedroom, she sat on her bed, overwhelmed by the things she had to do. Telephone Victor's bank on The Strand and tell them about his accident. Speak to his lawyer about the implications. Ring Laura and ask for yet another week, or even more, away from Hampstead. See the Chandos housekeeper about her plans for the week ahead. Tell the St John's Wood staff that Victor would not be back with them for perhaps a very long time. Make sure their groom had been given the help he needed for the disposal of poor Domino.

The list of chores went on and on as her energy evaporated.

She tore at the envelope.

Theo's cottage   *Tuesday afternoon*

My darling girl

By the time you read this letter, I shall be on the train to London. I shall not be coming back to Charlbury. My English sabbatical has turned into a nightmare of anxiety and longing. You have just come from the bedside of a man whose life, in my heart, I did not want to save. But I knew I had to bring him home to you.

I am leaving Hermione for you as a gift. I hope that when you sit behind the wheel again, you will think of me, and of the marvellous hours we spent in her together. Remember everything I taught you and drive carefully.

I know that in loving you, in giving you our child, I not only

221

stepped over the line, but I turned our tiny paradise into a dangerous summer. Yet, given the choice, I would do it all again for those few miraculous hours of love we were lucky enough to share.

Please forgive me, but do not forget.

I hope with all my heart that we shall, one day, meet again.

Ever your own, with all my love
Alex

'You must take all the time you need,' Laura said.

Laura had caught the train to Charlbury on Saturday morning and now walked in the gardens with her beloved friend.

'We're just about managing without you. The girls send their love. Luckily, many of our clients are on holiday. The autumn rush won't begin for another couple of weeks.'

'The worst thing,' Beatrice told her, 'is that Victor is still unconscious. I sat beside his hospital bed this morning, talking rubbish, but he's got no idea I'm there – and I might just as well not be.'

'The most important thing is *your* health and well-being.' Laura drew her arm through hers. 'I don't need to remind you what happened when Ralph died.'

'That was different. I was madly in love with your brother.'

'But you no longer are with Victor?'

Beatrice stopped in her tracks. She gazed out across the lawns to the river where Alex had found her husband. 'How can I be? Who could *expect* me to love someone who put me through such agony because he couldn't face the truth?'

She waved at Theo as he came galloping towards them on Diamond.

'Now *there's* a man who can handle the truth. About

222

everything. Nobody knows but you that I'm having a baby. When I decide to make it public knowledge, Theo's the first person I shall tell.'

Laura looked at her. The colour had returned to her cheeks. She'd begun to sleep again. A soft radiance had crept into her eyes.

'And what exactly will you tell him, Bea? That his original plan for your body eventually succeeded? That Victor will make a wonderful doting father? Or that Theo's own brother from across the seas has left his baby with you?'

'I've no idea. You'd better ask me again in six months' time when I can no longer keep my secret.'

For the loneliest ten days of her life, Beatrice maintained her vigil at Victor's hospital bed. He showed no signs of recovery. His doctors could give her no reassurances of any kind.

But when the telephone rang late one night in Chandos, and she'd flung herself out of bed and downstairs to the hall to answer it, the news came as a shock.

'I'm so sorry to have to tell you, Mrs Davenport.' The voice from Oxford sounded cool and calm. 'In spite of our best efforts, your husband died peacefully in his sleep half an hour ago. I know you will understand that we did everything in our power to keep him well. If you'd care to come and see him in the morning, we will of course be supportive in every way. We send you our deepest sympathy and sincere condolences.'

It seemed that half of Charlbury attended Victor's funeral.

People came from the village itself, from Woodstock and Chipping Norton and Oxford, and from London: fishermen friends and neighbours, business colleagues and banking associates. They crowded into the tiny church on the edge of Chandos Manor, filling it with flowers and hymns and lusty voices singing.

Then they piled out of the church and into Chandos Manor's gardens, eating their way through mounds of sandwiches and cakes, drinking gallons of iced punch and piping hot tea.

Even Miriam came with Emile in tow, and Charlotte and Foxie – and her ever-faithful Laura and a stunningly turned-out Theo.

By three o'clock, her hand aching, her head throbbing and her face stiff from smiling acknowledgement, she sat down at the table in the middle of the lawn.

Apart from Laura she was at long last alone.

She reached across and took her best friend's hand.

'I've spoken to Victor's lawyers. I've decided to sell Chandos. Some neighbours of ours want to buy it, lock, stock and barrel. Theo will be allowed to ride the horses whenever he wants. I shall rent out the house in St John's Wood, complete with its housekeeper and servants – and even my maid.'

She smiled through her tears.

'I know you'll be delighted to hear that I'm coming home to Hampstead and the house where I was born … There will be three of us: me, the baby and Hermione. Our chauffeur has agreed to drive the Rolls to London with us tomorrow. We'll park her in Elm Row. I'll learn to navigate the streets of London without Alex by my side.'

'Does he know about Victor?'

'I asked Theo to write to New York and tell him.'

'Aren't you going to write to him yourself?'

'And tell him what, Laura? That I'm still in love with him? I miss him every moment of the day and half the night? I sleep with his letter underneath my pillow? I can hardly walk past Theo's cottage without bursting into tears?'

She clasped Laura's hands.

'I have to look forward. With the money from Chandos we can expand our little enterprise. We'll take on two more girls. I want to design a new collection of dresses for pregnant women. To convert my father's bedroom into a wonderful nursery. And I want to stay plump and healthy, ready and waiting for the new arrival.'

'I'll drink to that,' Laura said. 'Is there any champagne left?'

One afternoon in October a slim, dark-haired girl who looked older than her years knocked on the door of *A Passion for Fashion* and stood waiting for it to open.

'Charlotte! How wonderful to see you again.'

'Is it convenient, Auntie Bea? I know you often have clients at this time of day.'

'It's perfect.' She helped Charlotte slip off her coat and hat. 'I have an unusually free afternoon and you'll help to fill it.'

'The thing is, I've come as a proper client.' Charlotte blushed. 'My Uncle Jonathan is here on leave from Calcutta. He's staying with us in Kensington. He's invited me to sail with him to India next month, and I've agreed.'

'But that's wonderful! You'll have the most extraordinary time. I've several clients who've been there and come back with such stories you would not believe.'

'It would suit me to go … I'm not the slightest bit happy living with Miriam. She's often said she doesn't know what to do with me, and she's constantly terrified that I might run away again.'

Charlotte twisted her hands together.

'I know it was a stupid thing to do and I'm sorry. I made

a complete fool of myself with Dr Hertzler. I only hope he's forgotten all about me. Going to India will be a big adventure. I'll make new friends, live a different kind of life. I can hardly wait.'

'And you'll need a completely new wardrobe for all those parties in all that heat … New underwear … Everything.' Beatrice held out her hand. 'Come into my study. I can show you some designs I created last year for one of my friends. She's still out in Delhi. You can choose whatever you like from her collection.'

'You do realise,' Charlotte bit her lip, 'I won't be presented at Court next spring, so I won't need dresses for that. They call us girls the Fishing Fleet because we're all supposed to find a husband on the trip … If we fail to find one and come home, we're called a Returned Empty.'

'And *that*,' said her aunt, 'is the very last thing in the world that will ever happen to *you*!' She hugged her niece. 'Especially, darling, in my gorgeous frocks.'

The following morning Beatrice hailed a cab to take her to Harley Street.

She remembered visiting Theo that May morning more than a year ago. Now most of the trees in Regent's Park stood bare. Their leaves had fallen early in the summer's drought, lying in piles of red and gold in every dusty corner of the city.

This morning was so entirely different. Theo looked across his desk at her, his eyes shining with excitement and triumph.

'Congratulations, Beatrice! I confirm you have an April baby on the way. Everything looks to be in its proper place. I'm so delighted.'

'Thank you, Theo … Your advice certainly helped me to slow down.'

'And well done to Victor, too. Did you manage to tell him you were pregnant before the tragic accident?'

'I'm afraid not.' Her mouth tasted of bitter lemons. There are white lies and black lies. Then there are lies of every hue. 'I didn't want to tell him before I was sure.'

'That's terribly sad. So now we have a double duty to make sure everything goes according to plan. Let me look after you until the birth, which I'll attend.'

'Thank you so much, Theo. If it hadn't been for you – ' If it hadn't been for Theo, none of this would have happened. He'd brought Alex to England. He'd driven him to Charlbury. He'd lent Alex his cottage, allowed him to take it over. Theo's wonderful American voice reminded her of Alex. He was, of course, still Alex's brother. Cactus-spiked tears pricked her eyes.

'If it hadn't been for you, I'd still be praying for a miracle.'

Theo stood up and held out his hand.

'You know, Beatrice, Charlbury's not the same without the Davenports. Of course, I ride the Chandos horses, but I haven't been inside the house since Victor's funeral … I miss you both tremendously … Will you let me take you to dinner one evening? Just for old times' sake?'

Beatrice discovered that Theo was excellent company.

All through that autumn, old times' sake became a regular evening event. Theo would pick her up in his sports car and whizz her off to a small restaurant in town. They'd eat and drink and talk nineteen to the dozen, and then he'd whizz her home.

Except that one Friday night in December, something changed. She saw a seriousness of purpose in Theo's eyes she'd never noticed before.

After they'd eaten and were sitting with tiny cups of

coffee, he said, 'I wanted to ask you something. Some friends of mine live in Edinburgh. I stayed with them in the summer. They've invited me to spend Christmas with them.'

He smiled at her, his eyes dark, his skin glowing, his voice husky with hesitation.

'I wondered whether you'd like to come with me.'

She caught her breath. 'Theo! What a wonderful invitation. But I can't possibly leave Laura on her own – '

'I thought you'd say that.' He glanced down at the table. 'Actually, if the truth be told, I wanted to ask you something else. I've grown to love you very much and I want you to be my wife. I know the baby is Victor's, but I'd love it just as much as if it were really mine. Would you do me the honour and marry me?'

Without a moment's second thought, she said, 'My dearest Theo, don't you understand? Haven't you guessed? You're already my baby's uncle.'

Theo stared at her, his coffee cup in mid-air, his eyes wide.

'You can't mean what I think you mean.'

'I absolutely do. Alex and I fell in love the first evening we met … Don't you remember? Charlotte was taken ill. Alex drove us to the Radcliffe in Victor's Daimler. I told you your brother had been the hero of the hour.'

Theo's cup rattled as he put it down.

'So you did … Well, I'll be damned … Alex spent the entire summer at Charlbury. He had all the time in the world – and then he also had you. He never gave me the slightest hint he was in love with you.'

'Nothing happened for weeks, Theo. Neither of us would let anything actually happen. Until one blazing afternoon, when it finally did.'

'Does he know about the baby?'

'Yes. He knew as soon as I did. And then I had to pretend

to Victor, and everything quickly became impossible.'

'And now? What do you feel about my brother now?'

She clasped her hands together in her lap so tightly her nails bit into her skin.

'I love him as I've never loved anyone before.'

'You do know he and Lillian are now divorced.'

'No.' Her heart leaped into her throat and almost strangled her. 'We've never written to each other, not since he left for New York ... I'd no idea.'

Theo leaned back in his chair, his eyes on hers.

'Well, then, my dearest Beatrice. We'd better do something about this, hadn't we? ... What do you have in your diary next year around the end of May?'

Alexander

Alex clumped up the steps of his brownstone house and opened the door.

He could hardly believe he was back in New York. Nothing had changed and yet everything had changed. He was the same man, and yet he felt as if he were an entirely different person, looking at the world with a pair of new and shining eyes.

He dumped his suitcase in the hall and raced immediately around the house, opening all the doors and windows, allowing the early autumn air to dance into every nook and cranny. The kitchen and bathroom were spotless. Every surface shone. Someone had stashed milk, eggs, bread, cheese and coffee beans in the gleaming pantry. A card stood on the table.

Welcome home! Missed you loads. Love Len.

Tears of relief and happiness stung his new eyes.

All yesterday's ghosts had well and truly fled.

The only room he found difficult to look at was Sylvia's nursery. Mattie still sat rosy-cheeked on the patchwork quilt.

Alex picked her up and plonked a kiss on her china forehead. Then he packed her away in one of the toy-filled cupboards.

Within the space of an hour, he'd unpacked his suitcase, sorted the dirty clothes from the clean, turned back his bed linen to let it air, rung Len at St Luke's and spoken to Lillian's lawyer. Then he threw on his oldest pair of trousers, a sloppy shirt and shabby sneakers, and went for a sweaty jog in Central Park.

By the beginning of the following week, he was back at St Luke's, telling everyone what a marvellous summer he'd spent in England, how taking a sabbatical was excellent for the spirit and the soul.

Every night he went to sleep thinking of Beatrice Davenport. His dreams were haunted by her face, her hands, her voice. Every dawn he woke refreshed to tackle another day with only her memory to feed him.

He was determined to maintain the standards of the brownstone house that now, after his divorce, belonged to him. He hired a part-time housekeeper. He paid every bill the moment he opened it. His work at St Luke's improved out of all recognition.

The sight and smell of alcohol made him want to vomit. He never went out alone at night.

After their civilised divorce, Lillian had married again: a lawyer she'd met in Rome. Her father had died, her mother was living with her. They'd met twice in New York before she'd left. She was still dark-haired and beautiful, but every time he looked at her, all he could see was Beatrice.

He danced with all the girls at Len's delightful wedding and gave a brilliant speech as his best man. He made sure that on those special days which brought back memories of Lillian and Sylvia – his October birthday, Thanksgiving,

Christmas, New Year's Eve – he was firmly booked at St Luke's, working instead of celebrating, deliberately avoiding the booze and the girls.

There was only one ghastly evening when he came perilously close to undoing all his good work and hurling himself back to square one.

In the middle of January he walked home from the subway one Friday evening as the first flakes of snow began to shower the street.

By Saturday morning the deadly quiet outside spoke of drifts of the settled killer. The phone lines collapsed. On a bitterly cold midday Sunday, he struggled out to the nearest store to buy food and a bottle of vodka. Back home he flung himself into a whirl of activity, washing clothes, clearing snow from the front steps, cooking lunch and making himself swallow it. Every so often he stared longingly at the unopened bottle. It stared back.

At six o'clock he had a bath and slithered downstairs in his robe, his hair wet, his heart throbbing. He went straight to the bottle, opened it and poured an inch of the colourless, innocent-looking liquid into a glass.

The telephone jangled into startled life.

He jumped at the sound. Some of the alcohol spattered his hand. He went to answer the phone.

'Al? It's me, Len. Just checking you're OK, what with the goddam snow and all.'

Alex wiped his wet hand on his robe. He could smell the stink of vodka and wanted to vomit. He found his voice.

'I'm fine, Len. Thanks for ringing … See you tomorrow.'

He walked slowly into the kitchen, where he poured the contents of his glass and the bottle into the sink, listening as the liquid glugged noisily down the drain.

He had no idea how Beatrice was. Every Sunday without fail he wrote her a long, passionate letter, put it carefully on the pile in his desk, and locked the flap. On his calendar, he worked out when she'd be having his baby. The weeks ticked by and he heard nothing.

Until a letter arrived from Theo. He sat in the kitchen to read it.

The Cottage,   *January 1912*
Church Street, Charlbury

My dearest Al

I've just got back from a short holiday in Edinburgh and I'm writing to wish you a belated happy Christmas and a very happy New Year. As usual, I've been inundated with ailing ladies – but I seem to have had a string of successes on my hands, which is so rewarding, as I know you'll understand.

Although I am still allowed to ride Victor's horses, and being in Charlbury is just as peaceful as it always was, I do miss the Davenports. Village life just isn't the same without them – or you. So I have decided to sail to New York again to see you in the spring. I shall probably arrive around the end of May or thereabouts, but I'll be sure to let you know nearer the time.

Meanwhile, I send you, dearest bro, my best devoted love.

Theo

By the beginning of April, Alex had begun to count the days. He longed for news of Beatrice, but none came. He invented a thousand excuses to catch the next ocean liner from New York City, but instead he stayed put and went on working.

He cursed Theo for not sending him any details of Beatrice in his letter. He reminded himself that Theo had no idea there'd been anything between him and the lovely Mrs Davenport. He couldn't ask Theo any direct questions in case inadvertently he gave his secret away.

He was sure if Theo ever discovered the truth, he'd be furious. He'd accuse him of taking advantage of his hospitality, betraying his friendship, ruining his reputation. When they met again in New York, he knew he'd have to take the utmost care not to let anything slip.

He woke on the morning of 15 April and decided he could bear the suspense no longer. Hell and damnation, what was he waiting for? The oceans to freeze over? His own child to matriculate? Theo to arrive with details that would make him howl to the moon with jealousy?

During the night, his head had been filled with dreams of Beatrice – and now the imaginings included a baby, nestling in her arms, covered in a pale blanket, pushing its tiny pink fists into the air.

He made an excuse to leave St Luke's in the middle of the afternoon and pounded his way to the nearest travel office. Outside it stood a boy selling newspapers. *White Star Liner Titanic, Biggest Steamship Afloat, Strikes Iceberg on First Trip and is Sinking* screamed the headlines. He bought a copy of the paper and took refuge in a coffee bar to read it, his hands shaking, his head throbbing with disbelief and fear.

He was being warned to stay put.

So he did.

He'd wait for Theo, listen to his news, be as diplomatic as possible and ask only a few seemingly innocent questions.

In the middle of May a cable came for him at St Luke's.

ARRIVING LAST SATURDAY IN MAY STOP MAKE
SURE YOU ARE AT HOME STOP LOVE THEO

Alex got home the night before, slept for a few short hours
and rose to have a bath. He danced around the rooms
impatiently, like a starving cat, straightening the furniture,
dusting the already-gleaming shelves, grinding some coffee
beans in readiness.

Theo would expect perfection – and here it was …

At three o'clock, the doorbell rang. Alex stood in the hall,
clean, pressed and sparkling like a jewel in the sun.

He opened the door.

A graceful woman in a navy dress stood on the step.

She held a baby in her arms.

Under her white picture hat shone a pair of radiant
violet-blue eyes.

'Hello, my darling Alex,' said her voice. 'I thought you'd
like to meet your baby son. His name is Bobby Hertzler …
May we come in?'

Writing Beatrice and Alexander

People often ask me where I get my ideas.

It's a very good question. Without ideas, lots of them, a novelist has nothing to say. The answer is: from absolutely everywhere. A chance conversation in the street with a total stranger. Reading an intriguing story in a newspaper. A sudden memory. A birthday party.

Reading other people's work.

I first started writing *Beatrice and Alexander* in 2008 after reading *The Bolter* by Frances Osborne, a biography of Idina Sackville. Idina scandalised 1920s society and became an infamous seductress. Published by Virago in 2008, it's an enthralling account of a dazzling but bitterly troubled life.

The book started me thinking about the three different types of women: those for whom family is everything in the world; those who have children they don't really care about; and those who long to have children of their own, but remain barren.

My novel is set in 1911 when there were no tried and tested fertility treatments. The stigma that hung over women who married but failed to conceive was monumental. It blighted their entire lives.

My thread of research led me to a second book, *The Horse and Buggy Doctor*, by Arthur E. Hertzler, M.D., published in 1938 by Harper & Brothers, New York & London. It's the most brilliant memoir I've ever read of a long life spent in medicine. The illustration on the jacket and the few inside the book (which aren't credited, sadly) are at the core of *Beatrice and Alexander*. In their honour I've called my hero Alexander Hertzler, and it's his American story – if only a small part of it – that lies at the heart of my own invention.

I'm an author who likes to do her own research. Many writers have large teams of people buzzing around them, gathering facts, figures and all else besides. I like to stomp off on my own, often checking every blade of grass and counting the lamp posts, partly because you never know what you might find. But the early and late sections of *Beatrice and Alexander* take place in New York. I knew there was no way I could get there and start stomping. In 2003 I returned from a trip to New York with an early brand of the Covid virus. It very nearly killed me. I decided that air travel was no longer for me.

So, through an Agent I had at the time, I found the most brilliant American researcher, Kelly McMasters (kellyinbrooklyn@gmail.com). Kelly knows New York like the back of her hand. She read my complicated brief and understood immediately what I needed. Maps of the city in 1911, details of the then hospitals, records of medical training, what people swallowed when they felt ill: you name it, I needed it. For three months Kelly beavered away, sending me chunks of information she had patiently found and xeroxed on my behalf. And then more: stuff she thought I might need. That is the mark of the true researcher. They follow their thread in case it might lead somewhere useful. Kelly went beyond my brief, giving me ideas I would not have had without her. I cannot thank her enough for all her help.

Twelve years is a long time to keep ideas for a storyline alive and fresh. Other projects kept getting in the way. But my *Beatrice and Alexander* characters wouldn't leave me alone. By 2019 I had four different versions on my computer. I decided enough was enough. Do or die. I must either knuckle under and confront all four versions head on, or give up on the project and wipe the dusty, jumbled indecisive slate clean.

The reason I'd stalled at exactly the same point in all four versions quickly became obvious. Some of the novel is crucially set in Charlbury, Oxfordshire, and involves horses. Although I knew and loved the little town, I couldn't find an exact spot to place my Davenports. And although I can admire horses enough to smile and stroke, if you were to put me on one, I should fall off faster than you could say Dobbin.

And then something quite miraculous happened.

One summer morning on Monday 1 July 2019, I caught the bus from Woodstock to Charlbury to begin stomping around, trying to find an exact location. As I was wandering backwards up a hill in a vague early-morning stupor, I bumped into an old friend. Nobody who wanders around like that in Charlbury goes unchallenged for long. I told her what I was looking for.

'You need to talk to Sally,' I was told. 'She's great. She's our Vicar. She lives the other side of the Church.'

Within the space of ten minutes, I was in the Church, and walking around it with a mounting sense of excitement. On Monday 8 July, the Reverend Dr Sally Welch of St Mary's Charlbury was kind enough to let me walk into her back garden. It is extraordinary. The Old Rectory next door still has its stables. Tears of relief and joy filled my eyes. I had my exact spot. I had my stables. I had the sloping garden, the exact place of the river, the railway line and so much more.

Now all I needed was An Horse or Two. Or preferably Three. Not to ride away on, no siree. Just to admire from close up. I don't own a car. I couldn't afford to trail around the countryside looking for a set of stables that would probably be closed when I arrived.

But suddenly, there was Millie Coles, the marvellous Groom at Park Estate in Blenheim. On Tuesday 16 July 2019, in the blazing heat, I spent a glorious hour admiring Millie's steeds. Domino with her swirling coat of black, white and orange, now has pride of place in *Beatrice and Alexander*. I was allowed to stroke her. To look into her all-too-perceptive eyes. To see the cleanness of the sawdust on the ground the horses pawed. To hear their silent watchfulness. To become a part for a few moments of their utterly magical world.

So once again, here I am thanking Blenheim – and this time in particular my Millie – for the love, dedication and care that go into her work, and made mine possible.

The horses and the heat and the gratitude had fair worn me out. Millie spotted I was flagging. She drove me back to the Palace. I sat down with a coffee in The Blenheim Pantry – a perfect space to write a best-seller – and then hopped, skipped and jumped back to my desk.

By Friday 4 October 2019 I had polished the first 80 pages of *Beatrice and Alexander* and written a full synopsis of the remainder of the story. I set myself a deadline to complete the novel by the end of 2019. And I did it, with tremendous zest and enthusiasm. When field research works as well as this, it can be a novelist's inspiration. Perhaps I should send Domino a year's supply of carrots with my name on them. In fact, that's the best idea I've had all day. Domino, here I come.

For more details about Valerie's work, please see
www.valeriemendes.com